MARY ANN BRANTLEY

ACORNS *from* IVY

"To be a daughter of the heavenly Father
is to be a child of promise."

Darcy L.

Contents

Part IV: Autumn

Part V: Winter

Dedication

To everyone in my life who inspired me to reach for eternity; to those who tolerated me when I was intolerable and loved me when I was unlovable; and to my momma and daddy, without whom I would not be. They taught me, in their own ways, how to live and how not to live. I hope this book will honor them throughout generations to come as it is passed on to their descendants.

Thank you to Wanda and Lucy, who shared their old photos and memories.

Thank you to my husband, Steve for standing by me, believing in me, and loving me through the years. I will always love you.

Thank you to my children and grandchildren. You are my greatest treasures and I love you. I hope this book will help you to know your Granny's heart.

Most importantly, a huge thank-you to Jesus and the Holy Spirit who have guided, guarded, protected, and led me for the past sixty-three years and will stay with me always.

Prologue

In Tennessee, when Easter comes in April and daffodils are at their color peak, the boldest yellow petals shoot forth amid leaves of vibrant green. Each blossom brings hope and a reminder of how God's promises are forever renewed. That's the kind of day it was on Good Friday, 1952.

Momma didn't know it, but the day she gave birth to me ended the life she thought she had.

I've spent hours trying to figure it out. Every part of the relationship between my mom and dad was a mismatch, out of place—similar to acorns growing on ivy.

Daddy was a restless soul. During the entire span of his seventy-three years, he never found a resting place. Momma's wish was a husband to love her, children to rear, and a home of her own where she could stay planted and grow deep-reaching roots.

It has taken a lifetime for me to come to understand that when God speaks it into existence, it is. That's why an oak tree can wander and entwine, and ivy can grow deep, imbedded roots.

This book is based on my life as an acorn, produced from a sprig of ivy and an oak tree. These stories are painted with tints and hues of color to hide the ugliness lurking inside our carnal nature; but I promise you, every miracle and every spiritual experience are one hundred percent reality.

It is my prayer this book will inspire you to stop and take a fresh look at who God is. He is Abba (Daddy) to those who believe Jesus

Christ is the Son of God, raised from the dead into everlasting life. To experience a loving parent–child relationship with our heavenly Father and receive His promises, we must seek His face.

God loves and gives grace to each of us; but He gives favor to those who love Him back.

Part I

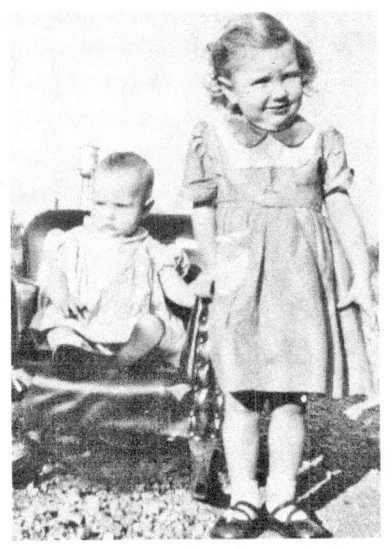

Chapter 1

The US Army drafted Cal Randall the day after his eighteenth birthday. From the hills of east Tennessee, straight off the farm and into the military, Cal's adult life burst wide open. Basic training pushed him beyond his physical limits and forced him into manhood, but he soon adapted. Freedom from the responsibilities of home and family appealed to him more than the restrictions of army life repelled him.

Cal did not want to stay a private throughout his tour of duty. The sergeant belting out demeaning orders humiliated him, to say the least, so he decided to move up the chain of command. Through twelve months of hard work, Cal climbed through the ranks of private, private second class, private first class, specialist, corporal, sergeant, and ended as staff sergeant. He had ten men under his supervision; all of whom ranked as sergeant, corporal, or specialist.

This is where I am meant to serve, he thought to himself. *Now I can breathe and think for myself. I give the orders now.*

Cal had grown up on a small farm during the depression years when food was scarce and personal possessions were non-existent. Everything had to be shared, and being number twelve out of fourteen children, the hand-me-downs were rags by the time they reached Cal. He wore breeches that were too short and covered with patches, and worn out shirts that were too big. His army uniform gave him a sense of importance and he liked that.

Cal deployed to Korea in 1946 before the uprising that brought on the Korean War and served among the American troops who helped train Koreans to be soldiers. The Americans had plenty of time for socializing with the poor and needy locals in the small Korean village nearest the army camp. The Korean women admired the courageous, bold, and impressive American soldiers who were so handsome in their uniforms. Many of these women held high hopes of marrying an American soldier and being whisked away to a better life in a more prosperous land.

That's when Cal met Soo Lee, a vibrant, diminutive girl with silken black hair draping gracefully over her shoulders. When she flirted with Cal and gazed at him with her dark, chestnut eyes, he thought he had fallen into a deep pool of heaven on a starless night. For nine months they basked in their self-created paradise. Their healthy baby boy soon embodied the passion they shared. He was a child from heaven with Soo Lee's raven hair and Cal's stormy blue eyes.

Cal's tour of duty neared its end. He hoped and prayed he could leave Korea soon and he began the application process for Soo Lee and their son to be sent to America. He had not told his family at home about Soo Lee or their son. He was afraid they would shun him. His family believed white males were superior to every other creature. Cal had no problem with having fun with someone he considered inferior to himself, but he had been taught the necessity of accepting the responsibility for his actions. If you played, you paid.

The scent of uprising hung heavy in the air as the villagers grew restless and fearful of the Communists' threats. Many of the American-trained Koreans joined the Communist soldiers hoping to save the lives of their families. Dark clouds of dread hovered over the villages. Rebellion brewed, and trouble lurked around the corner.

The uprising burst suddenly into full-blown combat between the Communist and anti-Communist citizens. American soldiers and villagers stood by near the outskirts of the village, helpless as they watched many of their buildings burn to the ground.

The Americans wanted to defend the village, but the conflict was civil, so the soldiers had orders to stand down. When gunshot rang through the camp, Cal fell backward as the force of a sniper's bullet rammed through his protective gear into his left side.

A few short minutes later Soo Lee stood watching as the helicopter rose, turned, and rustled off into the sky. She gazed into the heavens until the chopper faded away and the sky fell silent.

Twenty-Four Hours Later

"Where am I?" Cal asked.

"Sergeant Randall, it's good to see you come around. You're in the medical unit. You were flown here yesterday by chopper after a sniper clipped you in the side. We've removed the bullet. There is no permanent damage except for a small scar. You are a lucky man," the medic assured him. "You will be fine."

"That's good to hear," replied Cal. "How soon will I be able to get back to my unit?"

"You won't be going back to your unit. Your enlistment ends in two months, and you will be on medical leave for the next eight weeks, so we are sending you home." The medic flipped through the charts.

"There are matters that need my attention," Cal said. "I have a child and a woman soon to be my wife back at the village where my unit is stationed. Their emigration papers are not yet approved."

"You will be here a few more days. I'll see if I can get information on the status of your request for their passports and papers."

"Thank you, Corporal Grant," Cal said, reading his name tag.

"It is my pleasure to help you," the corporal replied. "I will order you up chow from the mess hall."

Two days later Cal forced himself out of bed to walk around the tent. He had to regain his strength.

"I need to see Corporal Grant," Cal said to today's medic. "He was checking on paperwork for me. Is he on duty today?"

"Yes. May I help you over to his office?"

"I can make it on my own. Show me where," Cal said.

Leaning on his cane, Cal shuffled to the desk at the far end of the medical unit.

"Good morning," said Corporal Grant, standing to salute.

"At ease, Corporal. No need for the formalities while I'm in my pajamas." Cal smiled and winced as he eased himself onto a chair. "I want to find out the status of the papers we discussed. Is there any news for me?"

"There is news, sir. A telegram came in this morning. I'm afraid it's not good. Because of the uprisings and conflict, requests for travel outside the country by Korean citizens are denied. There will be no further approvals for travel by Korean citizens until the conflict is settled. There's talk of war, sir."

The corporal could not have known that he had just delivered the news Cal Randall needed to release him from his unwanted responsibilities.

Early the next morning Cal received his orders to leave Korea. The chopper arrived at zero-nine-hundred hours to transport him to the military air base. Cal sucked in a deep, lung-bursting breath to clear his head. When the helicopter landed, Cal grabbed his duffle bag and shuffled out to board. As he climbed into the passenger seat, he wiped his face with his handkerchief, straightened his back, squared his shoulders, buckled the seat belts, and said, "Let's go." He fixed his eyes on the horizon and never looked back.

Chapter 2

Sixteen-year-old Belva gagged and pinched her nostrils together. "My lands, you stink. What have you two been into?"

Fred laughed and slapped his thigh. "What's the matter, Belvie? Can't take a little skunnnk oil?" he chided, drawing out the word as if to heighten the offensiveness of it. Harold circled around Belva fanning his coat, stirring the odor into the room.

"Why did you bring that awful scent in here?" Belva scolded.

"We've been huntin'," said Fred. "We got two rabbits and a squirrel. These sure will taste good with biscuits and gravy."

"Are you gonna fry 'em up for supper tonight, Belvie?" Harold asked in his Tennessee-Kentucky drawl while twisting one of her long blond curls around his finger and tickling her nose with it.

"I'm glad you got food," Belva agreed. "I'm hungry, and I'll be happy to cook them if you will clean them; and *take a bath!* Leave those nasty, skunky clothes outside!"

Belva and her two youngest brothers lived together in a two-room cabin across the road from their older sister, Minnie. Their whole family had moved into the cabin when Belva turned eight years old after their daddy, Robert, died. Robert had spent most of his life working in the Kentucky coal mines, barely earning enough to clothe his eight children.

Coal mining was the only work available for an uneducated poor man during the Great Depression. After the depression lifted, it was too late for Robert. He had worked underground in unsafe conditions for so long, the coal dust had gotten the best of him. It was never officially diagnosed; he died from black lung.

The cabin had two rooms: a tiny kitchen and a small bedroom– living room. The two boys shared a single old, rusty iron-framed bed with broken springs, and Belva slept on the tattered, lumpy sofa. When their mother, Nettie, remarried and moved out, their younger sister Lyla went with her. Nettie asked them to come along as well, but she never insisted, so Belva and her two teen-aged brothers stayed.

Winter seemed especially frigid that year. Paired with their destitution, the cold chilled both body and soul. Cracks in the cabin walls had been stuffed with old rags and newspaper. The tiny wood-burning stove produced little heat even when operating at full capacity, and though they had cut and stacked wood back in the fall, they must burn it sparingly or it would not last until spring. Their few old, shabby quilts and ragged featherbed were too thin to offer much protection from the frosty temperatures, so when nighttime came, they went to bed wearing their coats and shoes to stay warm.

When spring crept around, warming the ground and melting away the ice, all of nature gave thanks. Tiny heads of crocus peeked through the patches of remaining snow. Robins and mockingbirds sang a new song of hope, and Belva sang along with them, giving praise to God for His faithful promises. No matter what life's circumstances might bring, she believed His Holy Spirit would forever be her comfort. She didn't want to spend another winter in the old ramshackle cabin; she didn't know what to do, but she trusted her heavenly Father to help if she asked Him. So she prayed.

Dear Father,
Your name is Holy, and I am thankful You allow me, as unworthy as I am, to come into Your presence. Father, You are my Lord, my strength, and my provider. For all You are, I praise You.

You know our living conditions, Lord; and You know my brothers are planning to leave soon. I ask You to lead them into the life that is right for them.

I read Your Word, and I hear Your promises. Thank You with my whole heart for every promise You made in Your Holy Word. I ask You now to help me meet the conditions of receiving them. I give You my heart and my soul, and I will do my best to follow You throughout the days of my life. Please guide me to the next step You want me to take, and give me the courage to take it. I trust You, Lord, to guide me, and I will wait for You to prepare my path.

Thank You for hearing my prayers, Lord, and thank You for answering according to Your will for my life.

Amen.

*****

Bonnie and Belva had been good friends since meeting at church two years earlier. They spent many days together in summers past, talking for hours of their hopes and dreams. Bonnie thought Harold was handsome and sweet, and she loved the way he always smiled. Harold's playful personality never let him get depressed. He had been a real help to Belva after their mom moved away, and she loved him very much. She understood why Bonnie fell for him and was happy he and Bonnie were together.

In the summer many of the boys worked for local farmers in the hay fields and tobacco patches, and most of them squandered their money as soon as they received it, but not Harold. He was wiser in his youth than most young men and saved most of his earnings, planning for a better life.

Sometimes on weekends, when Harold had extra money, he took Bonnie and Belva to Knoxville to a picture show. When Bonnie talked him into it, her brother Evan would go too. He was cute and funny, and he always made Belva laugh. She and Evan had fun laughing, singing, and riding in the rumble seat of Harold's old 1931 Model A.

On Sundays, many of the local youngsters got together and walked to church. Walking, talking, and enjoying each other's company made the best of times, and it didn't cost a dime. They paired up as boy–girl couples and strolled along the graveled road to Macedonia Baptist Church. Belva's favorite times were when Evan walked up beside her and asked, "Do you like chicken?"

She would giggle and answer, "Well, yes, I do."

Then Evan would make a deep bend in his elbow, nudge her in the ribs, and say," Take a wing." She would run her arm through his, and they would stroll along together as the closest of friends.

"Belva? Belva? Are you in there?" Bonnie yelled, pounding on the cabin door. "Come and let me inside. I have something to tell you."

It had been lonely at the cabin lately because Harold and Fred spent most of their time working in the fields. Happy because Bonnie had come by to see her today, Belva answered loudly, "I'm out back. Come on around, I'll be finished in a minute."

Bonnie bounced excitedly around the side of the cabin to the back where Belva was hanging her few pieces of worn clothing on the fence rail to dry. She had just finished emptying the rinse water from the washtub around the rosebush when she heard Bonnie's voice.

"I'm so happy to see you," Belva squealed, running to Bonnie and hugging her. "What do you want to tell me? Did my brother ask you to marry him? Did you say yes? When is the big day?" she gushed, not giving Bonnie a chance to answer.

"Whoa there," Bonnie exclaimed, shaking her head in amazement at Belva's enthusiastic mood. "That would be good news; but no."

"Pooh," Belva sighed, disappointed. "Well, if not that, then what?"

"Well," Bonnie said, "my dad's friend Mr. Wilson says his wife is going to give birth to her third child soon. He told Dad he needs someone to come to Oak Ridge to take care of their children and help with the housework while his wife recovers. He asked Daddy if either one of my sisters or I would come and stay with her, but Dad said no because Momma needs us at home to help her with the gardening and such."

"Okaaay, but why are you so excited over telling me this?"

"Because," Bonnie said, looking at Belva with a questioning eye and a tilted head, "it's a perfect job for you!"

"Oh!" gasped Belva. "I never thought of that. Do you think they will want me? They don't even know me. I don't know them either."

"Of course they will want you! Daddy told them all about you and how we are good friends and what a sweetheart you are and all. Mr. Wilson can't wait to meet you. He says the baby is due any time now, and he needs someone right away," Bonnie said eagerly. "What do you say? Do you want the job? It will be an adventure for you, like in the movies."

"If your daddy knows them and says they are good people, I guess it will be all right to go. I do need a job and I need to get out of this cabin. So if they want me, yes!" Belva said, letting out the breath she had been holding unawares. "When can I meet them?"

"Let's go right now," said Bonnie. "He's still at our house. He and Daddy haven't seen each other for a long time, so they have a lot of catching up to do. Put on your Sunday dress, and comb your hair so you look real good. I am sure he will be happy to get you."

They stepped lightly on the dusty roadbed, trying not to get too much dirt on their shoes. They talked excitedly on the way to Bonnie's, and Belva became more and more nervous with each step. *I wonder how long they will need me to stay?*

"Here they come," said Bonnie's mom. "I figured Bonnie could talk her into it.

"Come on around to the front porch," she said, waving both arms toward the two girls. "I want you to meet Mr. Wilson."

Belva blushed as she reached out to shake his hand. "I'm Belva."

"Mr. Carr told me many good things about you, young lady," Mr. Wilson declared. "It seems as if you and I are both in somewhat of a pickle. I need a babysitter, and you need a job."

"Yes, sir."

"We can't pay much, but if you will work for two weeks helping Anna after the baby is born, I'll pay you twenty dollars. I realize twenty dollars is not much money, but I sure will be grateful if you help us out," he said as he gazed hopefully into Belva's chestnut brown eyes. "We will give you room and board of course."

"Twenty dollars with food to eat and a place to stay is a fortune to me, Mr. Wilson," Belva said appreciatively. "When do you want me to start?"

"The baby is due any day now. Can you go back to Oak Ridge with me today?

"I'll need to go home and get my things," said Belva. "And I need to go to my sister Minnie's too. I want to tell her I'm leaving and where I'll be staying."

"Good news then," he said as he extended his hand to Belva to seal the deal. "Off to the city we go."

Belva slid into the backseat of Mr. Wilson's car and told him where she lived. She was ashamed he had to see how poor she was but proud he liked her enough to give her the job. As they pulled to the roadside next to the path leading to the cabin, Belva breathed a quiet thank-you to God for answering her prayer.

Born in the 1920s, Belva never finished even her elementary school education. Students had to buy their own books, which were considered a luxury item by the poor, especially for girls. By the end of third grade, with no books to use and no shoes to wear, she had to stop attending school. During the three years she attended, she had learned easily to read, write, and to do simple addition and subtraction. Jobs were scarce even for the highly educated, and a live-in childcare position was a great blessing for her even if only temporary.

Belva loved the children, and they loved her. Her gentleness and patience made her a natural for the job. The Wilsons were very pleased with her work, and when one of the older children became ill and spent several days in the hospital, they hired her for two more months.

When the time came for her to leave, the children smothered her with hugs and kisses. "We wuv you, Miss Belvie. We don't want you to go." They all cried together saying good-bye, and she was sure she would miss them all. Mr. and Mrs. Wilson had been good to her, and their home had been a refuge after the stay in the cabin. Still, she had to go.

Chapter 3

The job at Oak Ridge was a turning point for Belva. For the next four years she moved steadily from one child-care position to another. During the short spans between jobs she, stayed with Minnie and helped her with her two daughters, Lacy June and Wendy Kaye. Belva loved them dearly; still, by age twenty, she had grown weary of the constant displacement. Her heart yearned for a stable life with a family of her own, but nothing appeared likely to change soon.

Change has a subtle way of weaving its way through our lives like the fibers in a tapestry. Each thread on its own makes no obvious, visible difference; yet when the weaving is finished, the pattern with its highlights and shadows would not be as lovely without any one of them. Change was in the making for Belva.

Whenever a financial need arose in the community, everyone came together to help. The most popular fund-raising events were pie suppers. Neighbors and friends came from across the county and gathered at the schoolhouse for a square dance and fund-raising party. Local musicians brought guitars, fiddles, basses, and mandolins. Those who didn't have instruments brought spoons and jugs to keep time with the bluegrass and gospel music, while dancers clogged, flatfooted, and square-danced until late in the evening. The women brought pies and other baked goods for auction and for cakewalk prizes. Rules required the auction bid winners to share the pastry with the person who baked it, so the bidding became a competition among the single men who fastened their eyes on certain available females.

"Who will bid twenty-five cents on this scrumptious chocolate pie?" the auctioneer bellowed. "Don't be shy, fellers. The lovely young lady standing beside me baked it, and you definitely do not want to miss your opportunity to share a bite of this. If the pie tastes as good as she looks tonight, you're in for a treat!" So the game was on, and young men spent their last dime trying to win the sweets.

Cal Randall won the bid for Belva's pie.

After the bidding Belva carried her pie to the table for two in the corner while Cal paid the auctioneer two dollars. Everyone watching them take the first bite made Belva so nervous, she thought she might vomit.

Who is this handsome man who wants to eat pie with me? she thought. *What if the pie isn't good? What if he doesn't like it? How will I ever get through this?* She blushed as he walked toward her carrying the pie.

"I'm Cal," he said, slipping into the seat across from her. He had neatly combed black, shiny hair and eyes the color of a stormy sea. Belva's heart melted into a goo as soft as the filling in her chocolate pie.

"I'm Belva," she said, extending her trembling hand to him.

"Don't be nervous. I promise I won't bite anything but the pie."

"Thank you for buying my pie," she whispered shyly. "I hope you enjoy it." She reached for a knife to cut the pie and knocked over a glass of water. Both of them jumped off their chairs and grabbed for a towel. They bumped heads across the table and stumbled clumsily, grasping at each other to keep from falling. Cal laughed until he cried, and Belva thought she might pee on herself. The harder they tried to collect themselves, the more they laughed. When they noticed everyone watching the embarrassing fiasco, they sat down and ate their pie, talking for hours until the evening sped away.

While the musicians packed up their instruments, Cal and Belva cleaned off their table. She wanted to see him again and hoped he would ask.

"I've had a real good time tonight, Belva," he said as he wrapped both hands warmly around hers. "May I walk you home?"

"I'd like that," Belva replied, looking at her feet.

So went the first of many evenings they spent together. Every Saturday night Cal showed up at Minnie's house to see Belva. They sat on the front porch swing, talking and joking until Minnie called time for him to go and her to come inside. Cal went, but on Sunday morning he came back to walk her to church. They spent the day together every Sunday, picnicking in the backyard or going for long walks through the neighborhood. After a few Sundays, Cal asked Belva to marry him. She had never been happier than the day he sold his milk cow for money to buy her a set of wedding rings.

They made their marriage vows at the courthouse in front of a county judge. No wedding and no honeymoon for them. They jumped into marriage full speed ahead. During the first year of their marriage, Cal worked long hours as manager for the White Stores supermarket chain, earning enough to pay the rent and keep food on the table. The only wealth they possessed was their love for one another.

Both Cal and Belva were excited and delighted when their new baby girl arrived in June 1950. She had creamy white skin as soft as velvet, soft curly hair the color of shiny copper pennies, and Cal's stormy blue eyes. They named her Belinda Lee.

For the next thirteen months Cal and Belva worked hard, and they worked together to make a good life for their little family. In July of 1951 Belva watched the clock, hardly able to wait for Cal to get home from work so she could tell him they were expecting their second child.

Stunned and dazed did not describe the expression on his face when she told him the news. He didn't say anything at first. Moments passed as Belva waited for him to smile, but he never did. With his mouth open and eyes wide, he said, "Oh!"

Belva couldn't interpret his reaction. Was he surprised or disappointed?

Over the next few months Cal came home later and later every evening. Stressed and tired from working longer hours, he had hardly any time for Belva or Belinda.

Late one evening a car pulled into the driveway and out stepped a man Belva did not recognize. He came to the door and knocked. Belva cautiously pulled back the cotton curtain from the paneled glass door and peered out.

"Mrs. Randall," he said, "I'm John. I work with Cal. I thought you should know what happened."

"What do you mean? What happened?"

"Cal is in the hospital, ma'am. He collapsed at work. I can drive you to the hospital if you want."

"Yes, thank you, if you're sure you don't mind. I will appreciate a ride to the hospital. Let me change the baby, and I'll be right out," she said.

On the way to the hospital she worried and prayed. "Cal is a strong man. What happened to cause him to collapse?"

At the hospital, John let Belva out near the front entrance and went to park the car. "Thank you, John, for bringing me over here. I do appreciate your help."

"No problem, Mrs. Randall," John responded with a great big smile, lifting Belva's countenance. "I'll come to see him after I park the car."

From the information desk the jovial receptionist announced, "Dr. Neely is the physician on duty today!" Her heels clicked loudly on the tile floor when she came from behind the desk and pointed Belva to the elevator.

The small hospital room held three beds separated by curtains hung on hooks along overhead rails. The other patients appeared unaware anyone else was there. Monitors beeped persistently, directing her attention to the tubes and wires extending from Cal's body like tentacles. She tried to slow her breathing and stay calm, but the sight of him lying there helpless and confined brought tears to her eyes. She walked to the side of his hospital bed and pulled the curtain half way around the railing for a facade of privacy.

"Cal," she said quietly, touching his arm with her trembling fingers.

His eyelids heavy with sedation, he blinked feebly and squinted against the light. "How did you get here?" he asked weakly.

Belva leaned in closer to hear. "Your friend John, from work, came over and volunteered to drive me here. Can you tell me what happened?" she asked lovingly.

"The doctor said he thought I had a mild heart attack, but I will be fine. He is sending me home and told me to stay off work for a few days. I guess he doesn't understand what it means to work long hours and still eke by."

"We will make it just fine if you work less," Belva stated matter-of-factly. "You have been working way too hard lately. We don't need much; we only need you."

"I want to do more than barely make it," he said. "I'm tired of working long hours and never having more. There has to be more to life than this."

Thinking the stress and sedation had him befuddled, Belva let his statement slip by without comment but not without notice. He never complained, so if he needed to vent, he could. "Will you be coming home today?" she asked.

"No," he replied. "Doctor Neely said I will stay overnight. I'll come home tomorrow. I'm not going back to that job."

"How will you get home? Is your car still at the store?" asked Belva. "John is coming up from the parking lot to see you. Should I ask him to come back tomorrow to drive you home, or should I try to get in touch with your brother?"

"Don't worry about it. I'll find a way home. You can ask John to take you back home as he leaves," Cal said and drifted off to sleep.

After the hospital incident, Cal changed. He quit his job at the White Stores and bought a small mom-and-pop grocery store. They moved out of their rented townhouse and into two small rooms behind the store. He kept the store open every day from early in the morning until late in the evening, and afterward he went into town with his cousins. Most nights he didn't get home until one or two in the morning. Exhausted and smelling of beer, he crashed onto the bed and did not move until daylight, when he dragged himself out of bed, grabbed his jacket, and left to open the store again, hardly speaking to his wife or daughter.

Belva didn't understand why Cal refused to talk about what was troubling him. She waited patiently, but he was always "too busy" or "too tired" when she tried. Belinda often cried for her daddy, but he didn't care. He turned his back on her sweet, tear-stained face and walked away. Belva's heart broke for her baby girl.

Two months before the new baby arrived, without asking Belva's opinion, Cal closed the doors to the store for the last time and said, "We're moving." He found a job in the city working in a mill and mine foundry; so they packed up their meager belongings and moved into a rickety old house in the country.

Cal spent most of his free time outside working on an old car or other busywork. When he did come inside, he played with Belinda and had little to say otherwise. Belva was happy Cal paid more attention to Belinda but unhappy that she and Cal no longer lived as husband and wife. She missed the way he used to hold her, tease her, and love her. She missed spending time alone with him, the scent of his aftershave, and the touch of his skin against hers. She missed everything they used to be.

Chapter 4

Her contractions grew stronger and closer, now only two minutes apart. Cal should have gone to pick up the midwife two hours ago.

"Mossie, please, will you check outside and see if they're here yet? My water broke, and the baby is coming," Belva begged as she scrunched over from the nearly unbearable pressure in her lower abdomen.

"Oh, stop being such a child," Mossie smirked. "I'm telling you, that baby won't be here for hours. I've birthed fourteen of 'em, and it takes longer than two hours, and more pain than you've had, to bring a child into this world," she boasted. "I see no need to bother Cal while he's working. Stop your whimpering now. I'll send him after Miss Ellie in a while."

"You mean you didn't send him for the midwife yet! Please, Mossie, when Belinda was born, the labor only lasted three hours; and she was my first child. This baby is coming now." Belva climbed into the old four poster bed in the corner.

When Cal first brought Belva to meet Mossie, Mossie gave her the cold shoulder. Belva dismissed the judgmental attitude and the sharp tongue as her way; but not so. Belva tried to get along with Mossie. *After all, she is Cal's mother, and since we both love him, surely there's a way for us to learn to love each other,* she thought. Belva soon gave up hope of being friends with Mossie and decided to tolerate their differences.

Cal's dad had died a year before he and Belva married and left Mossie to live alone on the farm. Cal visited his mother often, and one day he brought her home with him. He never told Belva she was moving in, nor did he ask if she cared. He just dropped her off, carried in her bags, and left her there. Mossie's other children convinced her to sell the family farm and move closer to town. The home place sold, but Mossie had nowhere to live.

Though Mossie had thirteen other children, Cal was her favorite. She called on him every time she needed anything, and he always ran to her when she called. Maybe he needed to provide for her, but often his relationship with his mother took priority over everything else. He and Belva had no privacy. Mossie was always there.

Most days Belva tended to Belinda and patiently tolerated her mother-in-law's disapproving looks and demeaning remarks. Today, though, she had to pray for more grace. The intense labor pains swallowed up her last bit of tolerance.

*****

Belva lay exhausted from pushing, but she needed to move the baby out of the wet sheets. She lifted herself by pressing one elbow firmly into the mattress and reached with her other arm until she touched the baby's body. She moved her fingers across the baby until she found its head and very gently turned its face outward placing a dry corner of the sheet beneath it. Her supporting elbow trembled and gave way as she fell limp back onto the bed.

"Mossie," Belva called, "please come over here and help me. The baby is born, and I can't raise myself enough to get her."

Mossie got up from her chair and waddled her four foot ten inch Buddha shaped frame to the side of the bed where Belva lay. "Well, let me see," Mossie sighed, exasperated. "You're not going to stop whining, are you?"

Mossie jerked the sheet back away from Belva and gasped, "Oh my goodness! Lord, do have mercy! That baby is here!"

"Will you lift the baby and lay it on my belly to get it up off the wet sheets?" Belva asked, but Mossie huffed and went outside to the porch. Belva heard her call to Cal where he was working on an old pickup truck engine for his brother Kent.

"Cal, I guess you ought to go get Miss Ellie now." She never told him he had another daughter.

Nearly an hour later Miss Ellie came through the front door with her midwifery supplies. She headed straight to the bedside to check Belva's progress.

"My, my, Miss Belva, you sure are a strong woman!" Miss Ellie exclaimed and pulled back the sheets to cut the umbilical cord and lift the precious new baby girl out of the soggy feather bed. "I've never seen anyone bring a baby into the world so fast. Your baby got here before I could get my bag packed. Why didn't you send Cal for me hours ago?"

Belva cuddled the newborn against her breast and smiled at the midwife. "Miss Ellie, God is so gracious. He spared me the long hours of hard labor. I had three or four hard pains, and the baby was here." She never mentioned her pleadings to Mossie.

Cal parked the car and then wandered into the room, surprised to see the midwife cleaning up the baby. "My goodness! Let me see my big boy. I've already picked out a name for him. I want to call him Leon. Does he look like me?" He took the bundle from the midwife and pulled back the blanket, his face beaming.

Then his face fell. "Another confounded girl!?" he rasped. "Good grief, Belva. You're not even woman enough to have a boy? Humph!" He turned and stomped out of the house, slamming the screen door so hard it broke loose from one hinge.

Belva's heart trembled within her. "I will not cry." She loved Cal so much. Why did he hurt her that way? Did he not love her at all?

Mossie asked brusquely, "Why is he so mad?"

"He's upset because she's a girl," Belva said, the frustration showing in her voice.

"Well, every man needs a son to make him feel like a man," Mossie snapped. "You should call this one Elizabeth."

"No," replied Belva. "A man needs to appreciate the daughters God gave him, and I'm not naming her Elizabeth. People always call little girls 'Lib' when they're named Elizabeth. I think Maddie is much prettier. There's a little girl named Maddie on the radio program I listen to sometimes, and she sounds so sweet. I like the name, and I've already told Miss Ellie to put it on the birth certificate."

"Hogwash. You should stick to family names. There's nobody in our family named Maddie."

Chapter 5

"Where have you been? I've been worried out of my mind." Belva couldn't hide her agitation when Cal came home after being gone three days without contacting her.

Stumbling through the front door and nearly falling across the frayed, tacky rocking chair where Belva had been rocking the baby, Cal cursed loudly, and Maddie wailed. Belva picked her up and cuddled her until she quieted.

Belinda sat on the floor playing with a cardboard box where the October sun haloed around her coppery curls. She squealed with delight at the sound of her daddy's voice. "Dada, Dada!" she gurgled and toddled over to him with her arms stretched high. Belinda stood at Cal's feet bouncing and reaching, eager for him to take her.

He picked her up and snuggled into her neck, kissing her under her chin. Belinda giggled and placed her tiny hands against his face, patting him with baby love taps.

"Give Daddy a kiss, Pumpkin," he said holding her close to his cheek. "Does Pumpkin love Daddy?" He laughed, giving her a big hug.

"Pumpum wuv Dada this much." She spread her little arms as wide as she could reach, then threw them around his neck and squeezed.

"Where's Mother?" Cal asked Belva without looking at her or Maddie.

"She's gone. Your sister Opal came by Saturday, and Mossie left with her. I don't know if she's coming back. She took her things with her when she left."

"Did you say something to her to make her leave?"

"No, she never spoke to me after you left except to blame me because you didn't come home. Why didn't you come home? It's hard taking care of the babies alone. I can't lift anything heavy, so Belinda climbs into my lap and into the bed. She's still a baby too, and she needs you. I need you."

"They made us work the whole weekend at the mill," Cal lied. "So I stayed in town with a friend. I can't be out working to bring home food for these kids and be here too. What do you expect from me?"

"But can't you come home at night? I'm scared when you don't come home. It's three-quarters of a mile to the nearest neighbor's place. How could I reach you if anything should go wrong?"

"I'll go over to your sister's place tomorrow and ask her to come and stay with you for a while." Cal promised. "I brought you groceries. They are in the car," he said, changing the subject.

"Did you pay the rent? It's due tomorrow."

"I'm not made of money, and no, I didn't pay the rent. Why are you nagging at me? A man needs to have fun sometimes." Maddie began to cry again at his snapping tone.

He placed Belinda back on the floor and said, "I'm going to my sister's."

*****

Cal had not been home for two weeks, and the groceries he'd brought on his last visit were gone. Belva put a pot of water on the stove to boil the last potato for Belinda. That was the last food in the house. She cried until her strength was depleted, but tears could never bring him home.

23

With Maddie in her arms and Belinda kneeling beside her, Belva fell to her knees in front of the rocking chair and prayed.

> Dear Father,
>
> I love You, and I am so sorry I've waited so long to ask You for help. You are worthy of all my praise. You promised Your children would not be forsaken, but I feel so alone and helpless. Please forgive me, and show me if there's anything I've done that caused Cal to abandon us. If he left only me, I could better understand. How can he leave his children? Please help him work out whatever is troubling him so, and please forgive him for breaking Belinda's little heart.
>
> Lord, I can't make this right, so I am asking You for wisdom and guidance. Please help us.
>
> This day I dedicate my girls to You, and I promise to do my best to raise them as Your daughters.
>
> Thank You for hearing and answering my prayers, Lord. I trust You are faithful. In Jesus' name I pray.
>
> Amen

Reassured, she searched her mind for a way to contact Minnie, who lived a few miles away. She could not walk with two babies. There must be a way. Then she got an idea. Maybe, even though she had no postage stamp, if she asked, the postman might take a letter to Minnie. They were on the same mail route and the postman had not yet delivered the mail today. He usually came by around ten thirty every weekday morning. The tick-tock of the grandfather clock on the shelf drew her attention as it chimed. Dong, dong, dong, dong; it chimed ten times. She needed to hurry. She found a pencil in the top drawer of the dresser, and the only thing she found to write on was a brown paper grocery bag. It had to do. She wrote hurriedly.

Dear Minnie,

Cal hasn't been home for two weeks, and we have no food. I hate to bother you with my troubles, but I don't know what else to do. Will you ask Ronnie if he will come over here and bring us something to eat when he gets off work today? I don't have any money, and I guess I'm a beggar, but I can't let my girls go hungry. We need your help.

Love,
Belva

Belva folded the note and hurried across the driveway to the mailbox. She stood there trembling, dreading to ask the mailman to deliver a letter when she had no money to pay. As she waited, she prayed a silent prayer for the postman to be willing to help her.

"Good morning, Mrs. Randall," the postman greeted her with a cheerful smile. "That is two lovely girls you have with you. God truly favored you with these."

"Thank you," said Belva. "I need to ask a favor of you if you can spare the time."

"Well, I will take the time. What can I do for you today?"

"I need to get a letter to my sister, Minnie. I hate to ask, but it's urgent that she get it today. I don't have any money for a stamp, so I hope you will drop it in her mailbox for me since it's on your route." Belva searched his eyes for a hint of his answer.

"I tell you what, Mrs. Randall. I will take the letter to Minnie for you, and we won't tell Uncle Sam anything. It will be my pleasure to help you out."

"Thank you so much," Belva said with tears of gratitude pooling in her eyes. "I will never forget how you've helped me. God bless you! Thank you again."

When five o'clock came, Ronnie pulled up into the driveway at Belva's. He and Minnie got out of the car and came inside with a suitcase.

"Pack up your things," Minnie said. "You're coming home with us. It's beyond me how any man can run off and leave his wife and young'uns without a bite to eat. God do have mercy on a man like that!"

"I love you, Sis," Belva said, hugging Minnie and crying uncontrollably. Her body quaked as she sobbed and sobbed.

Part II

Spring

Spring is the season when new life leaps forth in rapid spurts. Youthful seedlings and saplings vivaciously reach for the sun, never considering their mortality.

Chapter 6
Humble Beginnings

My first memory is of Momma, my sister Belinda, Uncle Ronnie, and Bantie hens. Uncle Ronnie built a wire pen and gave us Bantam chickens that laid tiny eggs the size of ping-pong balls, if ping-pong balls were oval. We called them Bantie hens. I was so proud of "my" chickens. Every day I gathered the eggs, and every day Uncle Ronnie asked me, "How many eggs did you get today, cotton top?" He called me cotton top because of my snow white hair, as soft and fluffy as a head full of cotton balls.

"Hix," I said proudly, or "heven," depending on the count of the day. He only asked how many to hear me say it. At four years old I still hadn't mastered the *s* sound, and Uncle Ronnie thought my pronunciation of six and seven was way too cute. I remember getting frustrated with him every day. I thought he didn't hear what I said, and I sure got tired of repeating myself.

Momma, Belinda, and I had lived in a camper trailer in Uncle Ronnie's front yard since I was six months old and Belinda was two and a half years. The trailer measured eight feet wide by eighteen feet long. It had no electrical connections, but that didn't matter since Momma couldn't afford to pay an electric bill. We used oil lamps for lighting. A tiny icebox was set into the trailer wall where we stored cold food when we had ice to put in it, which we seldom did. The sink had no plumbing. An open space on the opposite end of the trailer held a rollaway cot where the three of us slept together. The trailer had one door, and next to the door stood a miniature, two-burner woodstove used for both cooking and heating.

I recall two particularly vivid incidents involving the stove and my sister's mischievous streak.

"Now, girls, I need to go outside for a few minutes," Momma cautioned, "but I will be right back. Stay far away from the stove so you won't get burned." We had no indoor bathroom, just an outhouse, so there were times when leaving us inside for a few minutes was unavoidable.

"Okay, Momma," Belinda said.

Momma had barely closed the door behind her when Belinda went straight to the cabinet and took out a box of matches.

"What are you doing, Belinda? Momma said not to play with matches. I'm telling!" I said.

Belinda ignored me and picked up the little shovel Momma used for cleaning ashes out of the stove. She took a match out of the red, white, and blue matchbox, rubbed it against the stove, and struck it. She dropped it at once into the shovel and let it burn out, the instant Momma walked back through the door.

"Belinda Lee! What have you done? Didn't I tell you not to play with matches? Do you want to burn down this trailer with you in it?"

"I told her not to, Momma, but she did it anyway," I boasted.

"Both of you girls go to the back of the trailer and sit down."

"But Momma, I didn't do anything," I whined.

"Maybe not," said Momma, "but you didn't have to be such a smart aleck. You know better than that."

I ran off into the corner, crying, and Belinda sat down with a thump and pouted.

Momma had just cause for being afraid of accidental fires. Aunt Lyla's daughter, Lydia, died when their farmhouse caught fire and burned to the ground. The cause of the fire remained a mystery.

It was a bitter, cold winter morning; much too cold for an eight-year-old to wait in the barn at dawn, so Lyla left her in the house while she went to milk the cows. Lydia succumbed to smoke inhalation while trying to find her way out of the burning building. Rescue workers tried desperately to get to her, but the flames raged out of control. When they finally put out the fire, they found Lydia's body slumped behind the back door.

Lydia and Belinda were much alike, both fair skinned with button-cute freckle faces. Not so in temperament though. Belinda had a mischievous streak, but Lydia had the proverbial redhead temper. No one took her toys or jumped ahead of her in line. If they did, they most likely never did it again. She was a hair-pulling, tooth-gnashing spitfire of a little girl.

Another time when Belinda's mischief overpowered her, I became the property of Bayer—at least I could have been if branding proved ownership. We didn't own many toys, so bottles, boxes, and containers of any sort made great pretend dishes for our imaginary playhouse. That particular day we stood near the stove, impatiently waiting for Momma to finish cooking our dinner, and Belinda played with an empty aspirin bottle. She was in the playful, teasing mood she typified when bored.

She gave me a foxy grin, motioning with her crooked finger for me to come. "Hey, Maddie, come here. I want to ask you something." She stood with her left hand behind her so I couldn't see her holding the bottle against the stove.

Unsuspecting of any monkey business, I ran to her. "What?" I asked.

"Is this hot?" she asked; and rapidly held the bottom of the bottle against my cheek, giggling and laughing all the while.

Aaayyy! I screamed and ran to Momma. "She burned me, Momma," I tattled.

"How did she burn you?"

"She burned me with the aspirin bottle," I sobbed, looking to her for comfort.

"Let me see," Momma said. "Where does it hurt?" After she saw the place, she reprimanded Belinda in disbelief, "Oh! My goodness! Belinda! Why did you do that?"

"I was just playing, Momma. I didn't think it would hurt," said Belinda coyly.

"You come over here right now and tell your sister you are sorry," Momma demanded. "You hug her and tell her you love her, and don't you ever do that again."

"Okay, Momma," Belinda said with a cagey grin and hugged me so hard I yelled, "Stop it!"

"You let your sister hug you," Momma said. Belinda snickered and gave me a sweet innocent smile.

If anyone looked close enough they would have seen the word *Bayer* to the left of my mouth and slightly above my chin for several years afterward until growth faded it away.

Living in the tiny camper trailer with nothing to depend upon but God's daily provision, we learned much about His unconditional love. In the summer of 1957 I experienced my first encounter with the reality of God's love and protection. It was nothing less than a miracle.

The muggy hot day left the air so still, breathing stressed our endurance. Inside the trailer the temperature shot above ninety degrees, so Momma, Belinda, and I headed outside to find shade. Our camper home was parked among the pine trees where grass didn't grow, so Momma said, "Let's walk to Minnie's yard and sit in the grass. Maybe it will be cooler over there."

Uncle Ronnie and Aunt Minnie welcomed everyone into their home. Minnie planted flowers everywhere. Every spring, summer, and fall, colorful blossoms brightened the entire place. Soft grass and clover for the honey bees covered the yard. Uncle Ronnie kept bees in the backyard, and the honey made my mouth water. Their front porch had a wooden swing hung by chains from the rafters, a matching set of painted metal chairs, and a glider settee. We never doubted that Uncle Ronnie and Aunt Minnie were happy for us to be there, even when they were away.

Momma used to engage us in various activities to pass an afternoon. A challenge to find the first four-leaf clover and weaving stems from plantain weeds into tiny baskets she called grasshopper's nests always kept us engaged. The plantain had long, tough stems, so they were easy to manipulate without breaking. We spent hours outside entertaining ourselves with nature's magic.

Belinda and I frolicked barefoot around the yard in our homemade faded cotton dresses. Momma watched casually from the front porch swing, fanning herself with an old newspaper to circulate the air.

A sudden scream drew Momma's full attention when Belinda came running around the corner of the house, her sweaty face pale from fright.

"Momma, Momma! Come quick! Maddie stepped on a piece of glass, and blood is squirting out everywhere!" Belinda chattered on so fast, Momma could hardly understand her.

The glass cut a semicircle an inch wide, jutting downward at a forty-five-degree angle into my left foot between the heel and the arch. Momma grabbed me up and carried me back to the trailer, leaving a crimson trail behind us. She sat me in the yard in front of the trailer, ran inside to grab a pan of water and rags, and scrubbed my dirty foot until I thought the skin was coming off. She changed the water again and again as she cleansed the cut. Then she made a bandage from strips of white fabric, torn from an old bedsheet, and pressed it firmly against the bottom of my foot. Every five minutes or so we pulled the rag back to peek, hoping the bleeding had stopped. Instead it bled and bled and bled. Momma got scared when my face started to pale.

Uncle Ronnie and Aunt Minnie had gone to visit family in Kentucky, and the closest neighbors worked at jobs in town. No one in our neighborhood had telephones anyway, so we couldn't call anyone. Right on time a miracle happened.

"Go in the house and get my Bible," Momma said to Belinda. "Someone told me once if you read Ezekiel 16:6, it will stop blood."

Belinda ran inside and got Momma's treasured white Bible. Her teacher, Mrs. Trexler, had given it to her for being the best reader in class. Momma turned to the chapter and verse and read: "And when I passed by thee, and saw thee polluted in thine own blood, I said unto thee when thou wast in thy blood, Live; yea, I said unto thee when thou wast in thy blood, Live."

She read the verse over and over again and prayed for God to stop the bleeding. All the while, I held the rag against my foot, peeking from time to time. Lo and behold, the bleeding stopped. I pulled back the rag to look, and the cut was clean and blood free, looking as if it had happened at least a day ago. The skin had begun to knit back together.

"Look, Momma!" I exclaimed. "It's not bleeding anymore, and it's already getting better!"

We sat there, Momma teary eyed with amazement, praising God and giving thanks.

Chapter 7

We lived in the trailer until the summer before I started first grade. The three of us no longer fit into the rollaway bed. Momma had started praying and making plans for better living conditions, but God already had a plan. Before the summer ended, Granny Nettie's husband, Walt (whom everyone called Poppy), passed away. After he died, Poppy's children insisted on Granny Nettie not living alone, even though she made it quite clear that was what she wanted. Neither did Momma want to move in with her mother, especially knowing Granny didn't want us there. Circumstances, however, dictated it. Momma had no money for paying rent, and Granny couldn't convince anyone she would be all right alone, so we moved in.

Granny's house had two bedrooms, a kitchen, a living room, and two porches. It was small, but in comparison to the camper, the place was huge. We soared like birds loosed from a cage. Granny also had an outhouse, a barn, a pond, and a big old white, lazy mongrel of a dog named Snowball. Water came from a cistern fed by rainwater, and we drew it out using a bucket on a rope. The water tasted great, and when we washed our hair, the rainwater left it as soft as silk.

"Let's go play house, Belinda."

"Okay, Sis. I get to be the mommy, and you can be my baby."

"No, let's pretend to be mommies, and we can take our pajama dolls to be our babies."

"I know! I know!" Belinda's big idea exploded. "Let's sweep off the leaves to make a clean spot and outline it with rocks to make rooms. We can outline a place for a kitchen and as many rooms as we want."

"Yeah, Belinda, that's a great idea. I'll go get the rake and the broom while you gather up rocks." Belinda owned a real talent for creativity.

"Hey, this big rock over here will make a good table. We can pile up these leaves for a bed."

Every summer we spent hours and hours building and playing in playhouses with imaginary walls. The mornings flew by, and before we were finished playing, we heard Momma call us in for the midday meal, which we called dinner. The evening meal we called supper.

"Girls," Momma called, "come in and wash your hands. It's time to eat."

"I'll race you home, Sis! Last one in is a skunk!"

Jumping rope to rhymes and swinging on grape vines; playing with baby dolls, tea sets, and balls and jacks; and turning cartwheels in the yard—: those summer games kept us active. We loved nature's toys best: june bugs on a string, lightning bugs in a jar, and popping oak leaves over a circle made from holding your thumb and forefinger together.

On winter afternoons, we sat around the fire making quilts. Momma and Granny did the cutting and sewing. Belinda and I learned to thread needles and tie knots in the end of the thread and strung up fabric scraps. We called it stringing up "fishes."

"I bet I can string more fishes than you!" Belinda challenged.

"No fair!" I whined. "You have to wait until I get my needle threaded." Belinda didn't wait. She tied her knot and started stringing. Belinda loved it when she got a head start on the game. But not so much whenever her thread broke and she had to start over again. No one ever won the game, but we had lots of fun.

We learned to hand sew quilt pieces into squares and join squares into quilt tops. Sometimes Granny crocheted and Momma did embroidery. They made lacy table top scarves and pillow cases. After supper Momma read to us from her Bible and told us of Jesus.

Granny's house had electricity, so we used electric lights and a radio. We used the radio mostly for news and weather because Granny paid the electric bill, and she didn't get very much income, only her Social Security checks. Saturday night was special though. We listened to country music from a disc jockey in Cincinnati, Ohio. That station played country-gospel, Momma's favorite, so we listened to the Wayne Rainey show whenever the weather didn't block the broadcasting signal. Sometimes we picked up the Grand Ole Opry show from Nashville, Tennessee. I loved singing along with Belinda and Momma. We made pretty good three-part harmony.

We sang at church whenever someone came by and took us, and someone nearly always did. So we went to worship almost every Sunday morning and Sunday evening and to Wednesday night prayer meetings. Most of the time, we rode with our friend Jack, who drove a Buick with seating for five. His family filled the car, but he picked us up anyway. Even though we sat in each other's laps, nobody minded. Momma said God knew what we needed, so He just sent it to us.

Jack had a sleep disorder. Sometimes when he was very tired, he dozed off to sleep sitting straight up. Jack always sat on the front bench at church up in the "amen corner." We called it the amen corner because most of the amens came from there while the preacher was preaching. Our preacher was an old-fashioned one, who walked back and forth behind the podium preaching fast and hard until he nearly lost his breath. Occasionally during the Wednesday night service Jack dozed off, and the preacher reached over, grabbed his knee, and shook him until he woke up, without ever missing a beat of his rhythmic discourse.

We loved church. In the summer, if no one came by to pick us up, we walked. Momma did not allow any tomfoolery during church services. If you needed a drink of water or had to visit the outhouse, you'd better do it before the service started, because if she ever had to call you down or give you her special "I'm watching you" look, you

37

were in *big* trouble when you got home. Trouble meant a spanking or an "I taught you better than that" scolding.

Once I got tickled over something one of the other children said and laughed out loud. I got the "look" from the women's corner where Momma sat. I knew what I had coming, and on the walk home, I began to cry.

"What is wrong with you, Maddie?" Momma asked, concerned.

I couldn't speak for crying, but when I finally managed to stop crying, I said, "I don't want to get a spanking when I get home."

"Why do you think you're getting a spanking?" Momma asked.

"'Cause you said I could sit with the other kids, but if you had to call me down, I'd get a spanking when we get back home."

Momma laughed and said, "I forgot about it. You should have kept quiet, and I wouldn't have remembered calling you down. Now, because you reminded me, I'll have to do it."

She did give me a swat on the bottom because she always followed through with promised punishment. I sure stuck my foot in it that day.

Momma taught us to be chaste and ladylike. In our home young ladies did not speak swear words, nor did we ever talk about private body parts in public—or even in private. We identified them by code names. One of my favorites was the way Granny found ways to say what she meant, without ever saying it; like the way she taught us the proper way to bathe. She would snicker and say, "You wash down as far as possible, then wash up as far as possible, and don't forget to wash old possible."

Belinda and I listened intently to her instruction and giggled and laughed when we finally got it.

Spring meant Easter, baby chicks (doobers), and daffodils. Our church always held a big Easter egg hunt after Sunday school in the field across the road. Everyone brought two or three colored, boiled eggs. Just before the worship service ended, a few of the men went outside and hid them. Hardly anyone paid attention to the preacher on Easter Sunday. Everyone's mind dwelt on the egg hunt, but the preacher didn't let that stop him. The message lasted as long as ever.

Momma managed to save a few dollars each month from the welfare check to buy us an Easter dress, new shoes, and a basket for the egg hunt. I'm sure that to give us a nice Easter, she did without things she needed. She never bought anything for herself, not even necessities like feminine essentials. She made do. The rest of our clothing came as hand-me-downs from cousins or neighbors, but we didn't mind. They were new to us. The only contact we had with Daddy's side of the family was with Uncle Josh and Aunt Ruby. She made us dresses from time to time and invited us over for a two-week stay in the summer.

Once a year in May, Momma, Belinda, and I walked up on the hillside above Granny's house and picked wild strawberries. We usually only found a few. One year we found a patch of the biggest, sweetest berries we had ever seen. The patch was so big, with so many berries, we picked from the patch every day for a week. Momma made strawberry jam, and there were still plenty left for a great big bowl full of strawberries, sugar, and cream. Yum!

June always brought Momma's favorite flower, red roses. The best place to pick the biggest and sweetest smelling ones was an old abandoned homestead which once belonged to Poppy's brother, Otto. Momma, Belinda, and I walked down the road, crossed the field of tall grass—it hadn't been cut in years—and came back home with our arms loaded. We used Mason jars for vases and placed them in every room in the house. The spring breeze, frolicking with the curtains on the open windows, filled the house with the most wonderful aroma. If I close my eyes and let my mind wander back, I can still smell the enticing fragrance of red roses, fresh air, and Momma.

Most summers Uncle Fred planted a garden at Granny's place. I loved helping plant potatoes and corn, but mostly I loved eating them. Sweet corn on the cob with the homemade butter Aunt Patty made was so savory and so good, I could have eaten an entire dozen.

Chapter 8

"Momma, Maddie was crying at school today." Belinda called out before we even got into the yard. Our walks home from school became a time for Belinda and me to share secrets. We talked about things we didn't want Momma to know and made each other pinky swear not to tell. Somehow it never worked out. One of us always ended up telling her everything. Laden with guilt over whatever we'd done wrong, we either told on ourselves or told on each other.

"Why was she crying, Belinda?" Momma asked. "Did she get hurt?"

"No, she's just a big baby. She didn't have any reason to cry as I could see."

"Why were you crying, Maddie?"

"Because the other girls were talking about their daddies, and I don't have one, so I couldn't tell them about mine."

"Of course you have a daddy, Maddie."

"How come I've never seen him?"

"Well …" Momma stumbled for words and finally said, "You have seen him. You were only a baby when he left, so you don't remember him."

"Where did he go, Momma? Did he die?"

"No, honey, he just left. I don't know where he is now. I tried to find him once, but the only thing I found out from his mother was that he moved to California. She never gave me his address."

"Didn't he love us, Momma?"

"I don't know, sweetheart. I guess he didn't love us enough. I prayed for him and asked God to remind him we're still here and we still need him."

"Okay, so I guess he'll come back soon since you asked God. You always say God hears our prayers and loves us; so I guess we'll have to wait. I feel better now, Momma."

"Good, I'm glad. Now go wash your hands and get ready for supper."

The next year I was in third grade, and Belinda was in fifth. Union County closed our little two-room schoolhouse along with several others in the district and built a new, bigger school.

Big Ridge Elementary was the name of the new school. There was a room for first through eighth grades, indoor restrooms, and a multipurpose gym which also served as cafeteria and auditorium. The outside sported red bricks, and the interior walls were bare concrete blocks and mortar. The combination of anxiety and the odor of wet cement made little stomachs queasy but not queasy enough to keep us from enjoying the scrumptious hot lunches. At the old school we carried our lunch from home every day. If you were lucky, it was still there at lunchtime. If you were not so lucky, your lunch lay on the ground halfway between school and home where you spilled it when your lunchbox latch broke, or a less fortunate kid who had no lunch helped himself to it when you turned your back.

We rode the big yellow bus to the new school. In the wintertime riding beat walking except when the bus's heater failed. The old buses needed repair. On the coldest days of the year when we needed heat the most the heaters didn't work. By the time we arrived at school, our feet were wet from melted snow and so cold that our toes went numb.

At the old school we walked the half mile from our house to Central View Elementary. We owned only one pair of everyday shoes, and they had to last through winter. In the summer we went barefoot, except for when we went to church and wore our Sunday shoes. The everyday shoes didn't always make it through winter

41

without help. When the bottoms wore through leaving a hole in the sole, we cut out cardboard to the same shape as the shoe bottom and stuffed it inside to keep the dirt and snow out.

We recognized every car in the community, everyone who drove them, and what time of day they came down the road. Our neighbor across the road left for work the same time every morning and came home the same time every afternoon. Our neighbor on the left didn't drive, but her teenage son did. He sped through, stirring up road dust on Saturday nights. There weren't any close neighbors on the right, but several families lived a half mile down the road and drove by our house on their way to work, church, or the grocery store.

One autumn day, a brand-new pale blue Ford came up the road and stopped at our house. We had never seen the car, so we figured somebody must be running for public office or electioneering, as Granny called it. That's the only time we ever saw strangers.

"Somebody's here, Momma." We both ran to the back porch where she was washing clothes. The clatter the wringer washer made while sloshing the clothes back and forth in the tub had kept her from hearing the car pull into the driveway.

"Who is it?" she asked, wiping her hands first on her apron and then through her tousled hair. "I hope it's not company. I'm a mess."

"We don't know. We've never seen him."

Momma stopped the agitator in the wringer washer and stepped off the back porch to see.

She gasped. "Oh, my Lord, have mercy! It's your daddy!"

Belinda and I glared wide-eyed at each other. Then we ran into the house and hid. "What if he's here to take us?" Belinda asked.

"I won't go with him," I said. "Momma won't let him take us!"

Curious as to what was going on, we slipped out of hiding and peeked through the rooster-print curtains hanging over the kitchen window. We wanted to see how he looked. Momma stood in the yard talking to him, and then they stepped up onto the back porch, and she let him come inside the house.

"Come here, girls. Your daddy wants to see you."

Both of us lingered back shyly. Neither of us knew how to react. Finally Belinda stepped forward, and I walked closely behind her, holding on to her dress, afraid he was going to take her away from me.

"It's okay," Momma said. "He only wants to see you."

Daddy stood there in Granny's kitchen with a big smile on his face as if he'd brought us the biggest present ever. To me it didn't feel like a present. It felt more like bad news.

After he looked at us for a long time, he stooped down and asked for a hug. I didn't want him to hug me, but Momma said we should. He smelled like soap and cigarette smoke.

"What brings you around?" Momma gave him a cold stare.

"I came to see you and my girls and to see if you need anything. Have you been making it through all right?"

"Since you started sending us the ninety dollars a month for child support a few months back, it's been easier. The girls are getting bigger now and it takes more to make ends meet. God took care of us. We are doing fine," Momma told him. "Where have you been the last ten years? I tried several times to find you, but no one admitted to knowing where you went, at least they wouldn't tell me if they did. Ronnie talked to the county social worker and asked him to come by to see me. He's the one who sent you the child support order."

"I know," Daddy said. "I should not have left you to raise the girls by yourself. I want a second chance to do better."

Tears welled up in Momma's eyes, and she said, "I figured you would be back someday."

That was the first of many visits over the next few months. The next time he came, he didn't drive the new Ford; instead he drove an ugly older car. When we asked him what happened to the new car, he said he sent it back to the car dealer because it was a lemon. I'd never heard of a lemon car, and I didn't understand what he meant. *It's not yellow*, I thought. *It's blue.*

When he came over, he sat in the kitchen and talked to Momma. They talked low, so we never heard what they said. They sat close together. Once I saw him kiss her, and she didn't stop him.

We ate our first picnic lunch while Daddy was courting Momma. He built a fire in the backyard and roasted wieners and marshmallows. Granny didn't eat with us. She stayed away when he was there.

After his visits Belinda and I sat on the swing made from an old, rusty chain and a piece of sawmill slab we'd found in the barn and strung up in a tree beside the driveway. We whispered so Momma couldn't hear us discussing our thoughts about Daddy. Both of us were unsure of him. Partly, we were excited for the possibility he might want to be our full-time daddy and make us a real family like other folks. Mostly we were nervous. Things had changed since he had started coming over. It felt strange, and Momma seemed distracted. She acted like there was something serious on her mind.

The next spring, she asked Belinda and me to sit on the couch. She needed to talk to us. "What do you girls think about all of us going to live with your daddy? He is building a house three miles from here, and he says he is building it for us. He said you could each have a room of your own, and there's an inside bathroom, too."

We could hardly resist those promises. The old outhouse at Granny's was pretty scary sometimes and awfully cold in the wintertime. Once Belinda went into it and came running out much faster than she went in. A huge blacksnake lay coiled up in the corner. Granny dragged it out with the garden hoe and chopped off its head. For a long time after the snake incident we inspected the seat inside and out before sitting our bare bottoms down.

"Do you mean Granny, too?" I asked.

"No, Granny will stay here in her house, and the three of us will live with Daddy."

"Won't Granny be sad if we leave her?"

"I'm sure she will be fine," Momma answered. "She likes living by herself."

"Do you want us to go live with him?" Belinda asked. "What if he leaves us again?"

"We talked a lot about that," Momma assured us. "He says God told him he needs to do right by us. He wants me to forgive him for leaving us in the first place. Daddy is sorry. He wants us to be a family again. I asked God to bring him back, and since he is here now, we need to love him. Don't you think we should?"

"I guess so, Momma. When will we move?" I asked quietly, but my heart raced from anxiety.

Two weeks later Daddy picked Momma up, and they went to the courthouse to get married again. Granny said with concern in her voice, "I hope you know what you're doing. You remember what happened the first time you married him."

Chapter 9

Ten years of life as we'd known it evaporated in less than a day. We'd been poor but contented for as long as I remembered. Meekness, gentleness of spirit, and peace defined our way of life; and we were secure in it. One night in Daddy's house swept it away. *Everything* changed.

"Momma, I'm scared," I cried aloud in the dark room. "Will you come in here and tell me good night?"

"What are you afraid of? You've never been afraid of the dark," Momma called back from the bedroom at the end of the hall where she and Daddy slept.

"I'm not afraid of the dark. I just want you to come in here until I fall asleep. Please?"

"I'll come and tell you good night, but I won't stay. You can sleep in Belinda's bed with her if you want to, for tonight."

Since the day of my birth, I had slept in the same room as Momma. When we moved to Granny's, Belinda slept in Granny's room, and I stayed in Momma's. So many changes happened so swiftly that everything was going away and leaving me behind. I couldn't fall asleep. I needed to be close to my momma, just for a minute, for reassurance.

I heard Daddy speaking to Momma. "You're not going in there. She's a big girl now, and she will adjust." Then to me: "Maddie, your mother is not coming in there. You be quiet now and go to sleep." He spoke in a stern, harsh, and threatening tone. I feared him for the first time. I turned my face into my pillow to keep anyone from hearing and cried myself to sleep.

The next morning he called me over to him and sat me on his lap. "What's wrong this morning, Peanut? Are you still mad at me for not letting your momma sleep with you?"

"I didn't want her to sleep with me. I just wanted her to come in my room for a while. You hurt my feelings."

"You're exactly like your mother. You're too tenderhearted." I wasn't mad at him before, but I sure was afterward. I felt belittled. In my eyes he had insulted both Momma and me. Twice in the first twenty-four hours his words stung. I didn't like him very much.

That day started the beginning of a lifetime of stressful living. Belinda and I were both gravely disappointed with our new daddy. He never kept his promises of separate rooms and an indoor bathroom. The house wasn't finished when we moved into it, and it never was finished. He never did one more thing to it. There were no covers on the electrical outlets, no baseboards or trim, no interior doors or even door facings. Belinda's room had bare studded walls with no drywall or covering of any kind and it held unused building materials. The same was true for the room where the bathroom was supposed to be. He used it for a junk room. He had what he wanted, and nothing else mattered to him.

One day I searched through the house for Belinda but couldn't find her anywhere.

"Belinda? Where are you?"

I guess I called and called so long, she finally gave in and said, "What do you want? Leave me alone." Her voice came from the unfinished room where her bedroom was supposed to be.

"What are you doing in here in this junk hole?" I asked. She was standing there with her face to the wall, looking forlorn.

"You won't understand," she said sadly.

"I might if you'd tell me," I said, aggravated because she wouldn't confide in me and feeling as if she didn't like me anymore.

"Is it because Daddy never finished your room the way he promised? You can share mine. It's our room."

"No! I told you, you won't understand."

"You should tell Momma. You're scaring me."

She finally came out, but to my knowledge she never told anyone what was wrong. Daddy said, "She's probably got mental problems the way my dead sister had." Belinda was as sane as anyone normal. She had never been that way, and I hated him for making such a statement about my sister.

When his boss switched him to evening shift work instead of daytime hours, Belinda and I rejoiced. We didn't see him except on Saturdays and Sundays, and we spent more time with Momma. Whenever Daddy came home, he wanted Momma to himself, waiting on him hand and foot like royalty.

Our first year together as a whole family, we lived a semblance of the lifestyle to which we had grown accustomed. We went to church on Sundays, Dad went to work, and Momma loved being his wife and our mother. She was happy. Daddy still had those stormy eyes and the spirit of a rambling vine. He was never content and always looking for something to satisfy his restlessness. He started many projects, but his passion for them soon faded. When the passion died, he discarded the project unfinished. He was much like a Fourth of July sparkler; all fizzle with no bang.

We lived out in the country with no access to city utilities, so we needed a water-well. Daddy, being a man of many talents, decided to drill the well himself. He bought a broken-down but somewhat functional well drilling apparatus. The machine came without a motor to power it, so he hooked it up to the engine of his latest car, a classic 1959 Ford Galaxy hardtop, and started drilling. Day after day after day, that noisy contraption chugged in our backyard, dumping buckets of mud into the yard. In a couple of days we had a gigantic pool of wet, soupy clay mud right up to the back porch. We couldn't step off the porch without miring ankle deep.

After several days of drilling we still didn't have water. What we had was a drill bit stuck in a well shaft, embedded in underground rock, and a classic car with a burned out engine and dented hood. The huge drilling apparatus fell on the hood of the car and caved it. Daddy had to a hire a professional well driller to finish the dig. The final cost of the well, including the drilling machine he bought and the damage to the car, was more than the cost of two or three professionally drilled wells. Plus, when it was over, we still had to cope with the mud in the backyard for months, until it finally dried into a large clay mound.

*****

Two old friends of Dad's, Bob and Penny, dropped in to visit us one summer day. They and their family lived in Arkansas. How they ever became acquainted with Dad, I do not know. Bob lost his job and came to Tennessee looking for work. He and Dad sat for hours reminiscing and talking of how nice the weather stayed in Southern California. "It never rains in California," Dad exaggerated, trying to get us excited to see it. The more they talked, the more wanderlust set in. Daddy had made up his mind. We were going to California.

"We don't know anyone out there," Momma pleaded. "What about our house, and your job and the girls? We've hardly gotten used to this neighborhood, and the girls have barely adjusted to the new school. They made new friends, and now they're going to have to do it over again. It's going to be hard on them—and on me."

"You'll know Penny and Bob, and my brother William and his family. They're going with us. The girls are young. They will adjust. As for the house, it served its purpose."

"What if I say I'm not going?" Momma asked.

"I guess you will be on your own," he retorted. "I'm selling the house, and the girls are coming with me."

That's the day Momma realized Daddy had not changed. The promises he'd made, the house, attending church, all of it was what he used to get what he wanted. What he truly wanted was to ease his conscience. It had been nearly a year since the reunion, and already he was planning to go back to California. He must have planned it from the start, otherwise why did he say the house had served its purpose? We were excess baggage from his mistakes.

Nevertheless, we packed up our belongings and headed for California. At least this time he took us with him—for better or worse.

With the trunk of our old Ford packed beyond its capacity, we headed out. A few clothes, quilts, and kitchen utensils were the sum of our belongings. Daddy had sold the house to a neighbor for enough money to get us to our destination, and he sold a whole houseful of furniture to the neighborhood used furniture dealer for eighty dollars. Granted, the furniture was used when he bought it and not worth much, but the wheeler-dealer junkman hit pay dirt with that bargain.

Belinda and I didn't know whether to be scared or excited. After all, we had never been farther away from home than the annual trips to town. I guess I must have had more of Dad's spirit of adventure than Belinda. She and Mom dreaded leaving their friends and family, but I never gave it a thought. I was too young to realize California lay two thousand miles away, and we wouldn't be coming back any day soon.

Momma never learned to drive, so Daddy drove for four days, stopping for nothing but bathroom breaks, leg stretching, and quick picnic meals. Once a day he pulled into a highway rest stop and slept for a few hours, then it was back on the road again. Only once did he stop for a full night's sleep at a roadside motel.

Belinda and I entertained ourselves by reading the Burma Shave signs along the roadside. Each of several signs had one word on it and they were spaced just far enough apart to keep your attention. After you read all the signs one by one you had the message "Burma Shave is the best shaving cream on the planet."

On the drive through Arizona and New Mexico, a black ribbon stretched out ahead of us beyond the horizon. Except for the progression of numbers on the mile markers, we appeared to be continuously moving but going nowhere. Heat waves pranced in spiraling blue haloes above the pavement. Fences and sand hills filled the landscape for miles, and the only signs of habitation were the emergency phones placed at intervals alongside the highway. Every time I see photos of the *Apollo 11* moon landing, I'm reminded of the vast expanse of nothingness in the southwestern desert.

We spent our first night in California in a hotel, another new experience. The motel where we stayed while on the road gave us a place to lay our heads for a few hours of rest, but it never compared to the hotel. In all my eleven years I had never taken a bath in a real bathtub. Bathing on the back porch in a washtub was a far reach from the wonderful bathroom in the hotel. I remember asking Momma if we were going to be living there.

The next day we went to visit Harry, an old friend of Dad's. Harry and his wife Charlotte had twin daughters the same age as Belinda, and one son. They welcomed us into their home where we spent most of the day while Dad and Harry talked of old times and new times. Dad needed a job, and we needed a place to live; so while they got reacquainted, we got semi-acquainted with his family. Charlotte offered Momma a beer. Of course she had no way of knowing she was being offensive. Momma didn't believe in drinking alcohol of any kind, for any reason; not even medicinal. We found out later most folks in Southern California served beer the same way we served sweet tea. It was rude not to offer it.

That day we experienced our first culture shock. We had to ask them to repeat everything they said and to speak slower. I had never heard anyone talk so fast and have such funny ways of saying things. They thought the same thing about our Tennessee drawl. Their twelve-year-old son, Jess, asked if we were related to the Beverly Hillbillies. *Not cool!*

By midafternoon we were the new tenants in the house across the street from Harry and Charlotte. As it happened, Harry owned it, and it was for rent. Not only did he own a rental house, he had a friend who'd recently bought a house full of new furniture and needed to unload the old stuff. By nightfall we owned a sectional sofa with matching chair; a round, blond-colored coffee table (the likes of which I had never seen); a set of end tables; a double bed with bookshelf headboard; bunk beds; and a dining table with four chairs. The house came equipped with a gas range and a refrigerator. God sure is amazing in the way He goes ahead of us and prepares the way before we even know where we're going.

The day after Labor Day was a dreadful day: the first day of school. The school we had attended in Tennessee the year before had only three classrooms with two or three grades taught in each. There were three teachers, one who doubled as the principal and a total of around forty students. Everyone who attended was a neighbor, sibling, or cousin, and everybody's parents were acquainted with one another. For the most part, school and family went hand in hand, and all of your friends acted, talked, and believed the same way. Not believing in Jesus was simply unheard of in Union County, Tennessee. Not so in Compton, California.

At Franklin Delano Roosevelt Junior High, even the name was intimidating. Junior high was made up of three grades: seventh, eighth, and ninth. Each grade had eight or nine groups of forty students, so more than a thousand students attended. There was one large "L" shaped building with more classrooms than in our Tennessee high schools; two gyms with locker rooms and showers; an auditorium; several detached classrooms; a running track, a library, a cafeteria featuring a snack center with vending machines, and both indoor and outdoor seating for lunch. Everyone had two personal lockers: one for classes and one for gym. Showers after gym class were mandatory, and black shorts with a white snap-front blouse were the required uniform for physical education. Still more culture shock.

Never had we ever worn short pants, or even long pants for that matter. Christian girls in east Tennessee wore dresses, period. Only non-churchgoers and the unladylike girls wore shorts and pants, according to Momma; and a girl never undressed in front of anyone. If you attended Roosevelt Junior High, you would wear shorts for gym, and you would get undressed and take a shower before going back to your other classes. Culture shock, intensified!

Belinda was in the ninth grade, and I was in seventh. The first year we walked to school together, and after a few weeks it became easier. The weather was warm and mostly pleasant, except for heavy smog days. Before we left Tennessee, while Daddy was trying to convince us of the virtues of the West, he talked of the sunny skies, how summer lasted year round, and how it never rained in Southern California. East Tennessee enjoys four distinctly different seasons, so it was hard for us to imagine a place without winter. The first few months proved to be exactly as he described. Every day was sunny with temperatures between seventy and eighty degrees. Momma served Christmas dinner in the backyard as a summer cookout.

Then the rains came. For two months it rained every day. The rain puddled up on campus pavement, and running feet sloshed water up to the knees. We carried umbrellas to school and used them throughout the day between classes. The umbrellas didn't keep us dry, but they did keep us from getting drenched. At the end of rainy season, the sun came out again. Only a few days of warm sun dried up the moisture, and we went back to watering the lawn with sprinklers.

When summer came around again, the neighborhood had become familiar, but we still hadn't met any of the neighbors except for Harry and Charlotte. Cars rolled down the street and into garages, but the drivers were never seen. If people went outside, they went into their backyards, never showing their faces on the street. We lived on South Essey Avenue for eighteen months and never once saw any of our neighbors outside their home.

Our neighbor to the right sometimes spoke to Momma through the backyard fence. She never talked to Momma except to ask where we were from. Momma told her Knoxville (pronounced "nox-vul" if you lived in east Tennessee).

"I just love the way you say that," she teased.

Summer dragged by at a lazy pace. There were no churches close enough to reach on foot, and we didn't have friends or family to call or visit. Bob, Penny, and William and his family gave up on California. Bob went back to Arkansas, and William went back to Tennessee looking for work. Daddy took up golfing and seldom spent time at home anymore. He didn't let us call long distance to talk to family back home. It cost too much.

He worked evening shift in a steel mill. His shift ended at 11:00, but he never came home before 1 or 2 a.m.; then he slept until time to go back to work the next day. We had to be quiet to avoid waking him. No one wanted to wake a sleeping bear.

Dad was a chameleon. The same way a chameleon changes colors to hide itself from its predators, he changed his personality to blend in with his surroundings. When we lived in the country he became an old farmer; in the city he was polished and refined; at home he showed his true colors. To the three people who needed him most he was controlling, oppressive, and authoritative. Most everyone thought he was wonderful. In many ways they were right. He was highly intelligent and capable and whatever he put his hand to he was able to do, except tame the restless spirit within him.

His California friends liked to dine in restaurants that served alcohol, but Momma didn't. She did go with him though. He appeared to be ashamed of her. Once he tried to force Momma to drink an alcoholic beverage by ordering her a glass of Seagram's Seven and 7-Up mixed. He told her it was only 7-Up even though she was sitting right beside him when he ordered it. She never drank it, and when he noticed, he pressed her to finish it. She said, "It's doesn't taste good" and left it on the table.

I'm sure Momma prayed often, even though we didn't go to church. She stood strong in her faith and never compromised her beliefs.

School curriculum required a visit to a public library to get a library card. We had to find our own way to the closest library, since the school didn't offer off-campus services. The day Daddy drove me to the library, I watched carefully and remembered every turn of the route we took. It didn't seem too far. Then one day in the middle of summer, boredom got the best of me, and I decided to walk to the library. I didn't tell anyone I was leaving, because I felt sure if Momma knew, she would definitely not let me go. I thought I could be there and back before she ever missed me.

I walked three blocks to Alondra Boulevard, crossed the six-lane highway at the crosswalk, and then turned left. Two blocks over, a right turn, five more blocks to Compton Boulevard, another six lane highway, two blocks to the right and finally, destination, library. Twelve blocks in a car was a short drive. Twelve blocks walking alone through unfamiliar neighborhoods was a long and frightening jaunt. Halfway there, when I realized I was alone and a long way from home, I panicked. Then the Holy Spirit reminded me to pray.

Motivated by fear, I tucked my chin and began to talk to God while walking faster and faster toward my destination. "I'm so sorry, Lord. I've forgotten to pray for such a long, long time. If You will protect me and get me back home safely, I promise I will never do this again." As soon as the words poured from my heart and out of my mouth, I sensed Him there with me. With courage renewed, I continued on toward my destination. No way had I gone so far only to return empty-handed.

It had been nearly an hour since I left home, and the library was still a block away. Time sped by, and Momma was surely missing me and worried sick by now. I scurried across the final block, through the library doors, and straight to the fiction shelves, and then checked out two books from the youth section without even looking at them. I ran back toward home as fast as my feet could carry me. The traffic lights were the only things that slowed me until I set my feet back on our block.

"Where have you been, Maddie Randall?" Momma scolded, running halfway across the block to meet me. When she called you by your full name, you were in trouble. "I'm scared half to death and ready to call the police! I thought you had been kidnapped!"

"I'm sorry, Momma. I'm scared too. I went to the library, and it was farther than I thought. I won't ever do it again. Please, don't tell Daddy."

"Of course I won't tell Daddy. *You* will tell him yourself. You should know better than to leave without telling me. I would have gone with you if you needed to go so badly."

I didn't want to hear what Daddy had to say and was afraid I'd be punished; worse yet, he might talk hatefully to me the way he usually did, and then the tears would come. How dreadful.

When I told him what I'd done, he looked at me questioningly and said, "Whatever made you do that to your mother?"

"Will you take them back for me, please?"

"Give them to me when you're finished with them, and don't go there again."

He didn't scold me or warn me against the perils lurking against a young girl on the streets alone. He displayed no emotion, nothing. He didn't care.

The next school term, Belinda had to ride the bus to Dominguez High. She didn't talk to me much after she started attending high school. She had just turned fourteen, way too old to spend her time with a younger sister; plus she met a girl from Louisiana, who became her new best friend. They found plenty in common, both with Southern backgrounds.

"I'm going back to Tennessee as soon as I get out of high school," Belinda told me one day.

"No! You can't go back and leave Momma and me out here. You have to wait until we can go with you."

"I'm going," she said. "I hate this place, and I'm leaving as soon as I'm old enough."

I was afraid, so I prayed for God to please not let her leave by herself. What if she didn't make it? How were we supposed to stay here without her?

The five-block walk to school alone was daunting at first, and then lonely. I didn't look forward to going home in the afternoon. Belinda spent most of her time in the bedroom by herself, and Momma was always busy. Then I discovered the Golden Arches. Only two blocks off my beaten path, there was a tiny building where cars could veer off to the side of the street and order hamburgers and fries. I saved my lunch money, and once a week I'd walk up to the drive-through window and order a single hamburger. It was what I could afford; they were thirty-five cents.

The clerk at the window was startled the first time I pecked on the window to place an order. "Where did you come from? Don't you realize you can get run over out there? This is a drive-through window!"

I ignored her scolding and simply said, "I'll have a small hamburger please." Then rolled back the wrapper and savored the flavor all the way home. Momma would have been upset with me for skipping lunch if she had known.

The walk to school soon became routine and sometimes enjoyable. I could stop for a burger, stop at the five-and-dime on the corner to browse, and sometimes let a boyfriend walk me part of the way. I couldn't let him walk me all the way home. Daddy would have had a conniption if he had known my best friends at school were African American or mixed race. I identified better with them than with anyone else. A Tennessee country girl was a minority anywhere in Southern California. I was the only one at Roosevelt Junior High.

When rainy season arrived again, a girl from American Samoa had moved in a few blocks from us. Every morning she was pounding on our front door looking for a walking partner. We had a dreadful time communicating between our broadly different dialects. After school I tried to avoid her, but she always managed to catch up to me. Although I found it troublesome, Momma was happy I had someone to walk with. I'm sure she worried for my safety.

In 1964, when Martin Luther King Jr. and President Lyndon Johnson were working hard to secure civil rights for African Americans, rioting broke out near the mill where Daddy worked. Every day he passed through the section of town where the heaviest looting was happening. The drive to work had become a daily life-threatening event, especially since he worked night shift. We were sorry for the turmoil the rioting caused but soon glad it was sending us back to Tennessee.

We made the four-day journey back across the country, this time in a moving van with all of our furniture and belongings. Uncle Josh's house was a deliciously heartwarming sight when we pulled into his driveway right in time for Christmas. We were finally at home: sweet Tennessee home.

Chapter 10

Home was not the same as it was before California. Dad rented a house outside our old neighborhood, where we stayed for six months while he constructed another shell of a house for us. I finished eighth grade at the same school I had attended before we moved away, but I no longer fit in with the other students.

Old acquaintances no longer accepted me because I was not the same girl who had been there a year and a half ago. The girls didn't like me because the boys were paying attention to the "new" Maddie. The boys were only interested because of puberty. I had no friends.

Everyone teased me over the California accent which had replaced my old Tennessee drawl. They called me teacher's pet because the curriculum at the school in Compton was much more advanced than Tennessee schools, so scoring high on the exams was a piece of cake for me. I took a lot of ribbing and slipped into my protective shell to ease the pain of rejection.

"Hey, Maddie! Do you think you're better than us because you lived in Califooornia?" they taunted me. Nothing I did was acceptable, and though I didn't remember the earlier time when Daddy abandoned us as babies, the rejection still found its mark.

From the day I was born in 1952 until 1966, we were uprooted six times, each time more disruptive than the last. Belinda had attended five different schools, and I had attended four, never staying long enough at any of them to make lasting friendships. We had been both country girls and city girls, and now we were a mixture, so we didn't fit in anywhere. I blamed it on Daddy but never told anyone. I stored it away with the other unresolved anger.

When the house Daddy was building was far enough along for us to move into, we moved again. This time we were living behind Uncle Josh's place. This unfinished house had neither bathroom nor outhouse. We were forced to do our business in the woods until fall came, and then even the woods offered no privacy. Daddy did not care. We begged him to build us an outhouse, but he said he didn't have time to dig the pit. It is said that desperate times call for desperate measures; so Momma, Belinda, and I took turns at digging with a pick and a shovel. We finally managed to dig a hole deep enough to serve as an outhouse pit. He finally built the outhouse.

Daddy found a job at another steel mill, and again he worked the night shift. Since we had been back in Tennessee he was hateful, grumpy, and sometimes just downright mean to Momma. He resented her as if it were her fault he couldn't stay in California. Yet she loved him. I could never understand why.

He was never physically abusive to Belinda and me, except once when he was drinking. Momma didn't want alcoholic beverages in our home, but still he brought in a six pack of beer and sat in the living room with the beer next to his chair. She never said anything to him about it, so after drinking most of six beers, he started picking on her, making her cry. I'd had as much as I could stand of his arrogance and asked him to leave her alone.

"So you think you can tell your old man what to do, do you? Maybe you need to learn to mind your own business, Miss Maddie." Then he got out of his recliner and walked over to the sofa where he had ordered Momma, Belinda, and me to sit, like we were dogs who had to respond to his commands if we were to get our supper. He proceeded to pour the rest of his beer onto my head. Then he slapped me across the face and ordered the three of us not to move until he said so. Humiliation was one of Daddy's favorite tactics for establishing his authority.

There were many times when Momma took the brunt of his frustrations.

"Belva, what's for dinner?" Cal asked from his spot in front of the television where he reclined with a cup of coffee and a cigarette.

"I haven't cooked today, Cal. I've spent the whole morning canning the green beans I picked from the garden yesterday. The canners take up all the burners on the range. I will make you something in a few minutes as soon as I put these last few jars in the canner."

"Well, hurry. I'm hungry," Cal snapped, unappreciative of the hard work and love she put into her canning.

As soon as she finished filling the cans Momma made him a sandwich and a glass of sweet tea. She carried it to him on a plate and asked him if there was anything else she could get him before she went back to her canning, the same way a servant caters to her master.

"I thought you were making me something to eat," he stormed out at her and slammed the sandwich, plate and all, across the room, where it landed upside down on the floor. "I'm sick and tired of eating sandwiches!"

The only time Daddy ate sandwiches was the meals Momma packed for him to take to work with him. She always prepared home-cooked meals even when Belinda and I preferred something else.

"What are you looking at, Maddie?" he said with a scowl.

I stared at him and turned to go into the kitchen where Momma was crying.

"You get back in here, Maddie. This is none of your business."

Every time he mistreated Momma, my anger grew stronger, the hurt went deeper, and my store of suppressed emotions got fuller. *Rumble, rumble, rumble.*

"Cal, I hate having to always ask you to take me to the grocery store and the laundry on your off days. Why don't you teach me to drive so I can run the errands?" Momma asked Daddy. "Most of the other housewives run the household errands while their husbands are working. It could free up time for you. If Ruby can drive, then surely I could learn."

"Okay, if that's what you want. Come on with me."

He took her to a narrow country road where there was little traffic but the roadbed was a mess. Huge boulder-like rocks jutted up at intervals along the roadway, and drivers had to maneuver around them to avoid raking the rocks against the bottom of the car. That was Momma's first time behind the wheel, and she was an absolute bundle of nerves, so of course she couldn't maneuver around the rocks. One unsuccessful try and Daddy was ready with verbal abuse.

"Belva, you're too stupid to learn to drive. Move over and let me take the wheel."

He never gave her a chance, and he never let her try again. When she told me what he said to her, I wanted to pounce on him and rip his tongue out, but I kept quiet.

After the driving episode, Momma started going to the supermarket with Aunt Ruby. Daddy gave her twenty dollars a week to buy groceries. Momma was good at stretching a dollar, and sometimes there was change left from the twenty-dollar bill. Those weeks she saved the change and used it if ever the total grocery bill for the week exceeded twenty dollars. We had plenty to eat, and groceries were a minimal expense.

One day I heard them having this conversation. "Belva, where did you get this money in your wallet?"

"Oh," Momma said proudly, thinking he would be pleased. "That's how much we saved on groceries. Sometimes it doesn't cost twenty dollars, so I just save it over for the times when it goes over budget."

"So you've been stealing from me and hiding it?"

"No. Why do you think that? I thought you'd be pleased I'd managed to stay below budget."

He took the money from her wallet.

The next week, and every week afterwards, Daddy took Momma to the grocery store and paid the cashier himself. He spent more every week at the local market than she ever spent at the supermarket and bought fewer groceries. He never allowed her any money for personal use unless she came to him and asked for it. She needed a really good reason if she expected to receive any. He was in charge.

As with most teens, my room was my sanctuary. I was so angry with Daddy for the way he treated Momma, I couldn't think straight. So one day I went to my room and made a rag doll. I'd seen movies and TV shows about African voodoo, where witch doctors cast spells on people by making dolls resembling those they wanted to harm. They pricked the doll with a pin to mark the spot where they wanted the person to suffer. I didn't believe in it, but just in case it should be true, I thought very carefully before sticking the pin. After all, I thought, I didn't want him to die, only suffer. So I stuck the pin in the doll's wrist and said, "Here's a dose of pain for you!"

Chapter 11

Belinda married her childhood sweetheart one week before her eighteenth birthday. Even though during her teenage years we hadn't spent time together the way we did in the early days, I missed her when she moved out. That was also the year Daddy had his accident.

The ringing phone sounded out like an alarm in the middle of the night. Something was terribly wrong. Momma rolled out of bed and stumbled through the dark to the living room to grab the phone.

"Mrs. Randall?" a serious voice on the other end echoed through the nighttime silence. "This is Barry from the mill. Cal has been in an accident. We've taken him to St. Mary's Hospital."

"Get up, Maddie," she said as she shook me awake. "Your daddy has been hurt, and we need to go to the hospital. I need you to drive me over there."

"What happened?" I asked wiping the sleep from my eyes. "Is he going to be all right?"

"I don't know. They wouldn't give me any details. Do you think you can drive in the city traffic?"

I had just turned sixteen and owned a brand-new driver's license. Horrible as it was, I was thrilled to have a reason to drive my 1953 Ford. When Belinda turned sixteen, Daddy bought us a car to share. Our cousin Jimmy had covered the seats with rolled and pleated upholstery, and the exterior had a new sky blue and white paint job. She was sharp! By the time Belinda moved out and left the car to me, she had a few scratches, and her engine needed attention. She still ran though, and I drove her until she finally died.

At the hospital we learned the details of Daddy's accident. His hand had been severed at the wrist while he was repairing a broken lathe. My voodoo escapade came rushing back. The Bible makes it very clear that we should not mess with witchcraft and such black arts. Momma used to say, "Invite the devil in for a visit, and he'll move in with you." My, how right she was! I never experimented with evil spirits again.

The doctors and surgeons performed miracles by reattaching Dad's hand. When his wrist was healed, he still could use of all ten of his fingers. The only lasting damage was the stiffness in his wrist. He couldn't bend it.

The steel company offered Dad a financial settlement, a lifetime job in management, and a much bigger salary if he would stay. Daddy refused it and opened a used furniture store. That venture lasted only a few short months; then it was time to move again.

Tired of the hassle of working in the city, he sold the furniture store, our house, and the little house next door to ours where Mossie lived. He bought the farm where he'd lived as a boy. The old farmhouse was gone. A barn and a smokehouse were the only buildings still standing.

Daddy cut trees from the farm, took the logs to the sawmill, and built a roughly constructed, bare-necessity house. Momma said it was cobbled. The shack had two living units: one for Mom, Dad, and me, and the other for Mossie.

The only men who had ever been an integral part of my life were selfish, hateful, and controlling—or else the opposite: whiny, pathetic, and afraid of commitment. Yet there was a hunger deep inside my soul for male companionship and love.

A few months before we moved to the farm, my tire went flat on the drive home from work. I walked to the neighborhood garage to find someone to fix it for me. Stan Bristol was at the store lying in the back of a pickup truck, sunning.

What a lazy good for nothing, I thought to myself. I walked over to the truck and asked, "I have a flat tire. Is there someone here who can help me fix it?"

He grinned and said, "No. Daniel isn't here, and the garage is closed."

"I just need someone to take me back to my car and change the tire. There is a spare tire in my trunk, but I don't have a jack. I don't suppose I could talk you into changing it, could I?"

"Well, I guess I could," he said without enthusiasm. "Where is your car?"

"It's a mile down the road. I'll pay you if you'll help me change it."

He agreed to help, so I climbed into his truck and rode with him to where my car was stranded by the roadside. I admired his physique as the sweat poured from his head and shoulders in the midday heat. He sure was a handsome hunk. My hormones rose to attention, and unladylike thoughts whirled in my mind.

When he'd changed the tire, he said, "That ought to get you back on the road," wiping his brow as he threw the jack back into the truck.

"Thank you. I appreciate your taking the time to help me. I'll drive on up to the garage and leave the flat to be fixed whenever Daniel opens the garage again. What do you charge for changing a flat tire?"

"I wasn't busy, and I didn't mind doing it for you, so don't worry about it."

"Thanks again, Stan."

From the way he looked at me I was sure he must have read my face and seen what I'd been thinking. I was *sooo* embarrassed. I hoped maybe he'd call me.

He never called.

Stan and I attended the same school for two years, but he was ahead of me, and we never got acquainted. He was a friend of Belinda's husband, Jim. One weekend Belinda and Jim asked me to drive up to the Smoky Mountains with them. I said "No, I don't have a date."

"If I find you a date, will you go?" Jim asked.

"Who are you going to ask? I don't want to be stuck with a jerk."

"I promise, my dear sister-in-law, it will be somebody nice."

"Okay, but I won't go if he's not."

The next day Belinda and Jim came by our house and picked me up first before we headed over toward the community store. Jim went inside and came back out with none other than Stan, the tire changer.

Oh, no! My mind raced for an excuse. He was definitely not interested in me, or he would have called me. If lying in the back of a pickup truck in a public place was what he called fun, this was going to be a long, long day. I definitely did not want to get connected with a lazy man. Momma had warned me about those.

The day went by easily. We didn't talk much to each other, but the atmosphere was relaxed. When the evening was over, Stan got out of Jim's car and went home, saying only "Thank you."

Our next meeting was at Christmas a few weeks later. Several of us were getting together for a Christmas party, and we were each to invite whoever we wanted. Stan was nearly always hanging out at the store on weekends, and when I stopped in to gas up my car, I asked him if he wanted to come to the party.

"I don't think so. I don't have a date." He spoke as if he didn't want to go, and having no date was as good an excuse as any.

"What do you mean, you don't have a date? Didn't I just ask you to come with me?"

"Oh!" he said, surprised. "Well, in that case, I guess I can."

After the party he started calling me and taking me out every weekend. It didn't take long for me to fall in love with him. Stan's big, loving heart was exactly what I needed to fill up the big hole in mine.

*****

"I thought you said Stan was coming over here today," Momma said. "I hope he hasn't stood you up."

"Stan would never stand me up, Momma. Something must be wrong with his car. It acts up sometimes. He will call soon, I'm sure."

But he didn't. An hour passed, and still no phone call. "I'm going over there," I said.

"You shouldn't," Momma said. "Men don't respect a woman when she chases after them. It makes you seem desperate."

"I don't care how it seems, and standing me up is disrespectful too. I need to know why he didn't show up or call."

Stan was loitering there in the store parking lot with a big grin on his face. He came walking over to my car and said "Hello" as if he hadn't a clue anything could be wrong.

"You said you were coming over today. Did you forget?"

"No," he said casually. "I just didn't want to get out and about today."

"Well, you could have called to tell me that." My voice trembled with anger and disappointment. How dare he take me for granted! "I guess Momma was right then. You just stood me up!"

On the way back home my heart was crushed. It had been a while since I prayed, but the urge to talk to God was strong. I was totally broken. I poured my heart out to God and vowed never to trust any man again. "I can't take this anymore, Lord. I'm so tired of men and their disrespect. I thought Stan was different. If he's not, then I'm done with dating. I don't know what I'll do, but surely I can find a good church where I can work for You."

But God had other plans.

Later in the evening the phone rang. It was Stan. "Do you still want me to come over to your house?"

"Do you want to?"

"I shouldn't have done you that way. If you still want me to come over, I will."

"I guess it will be okay if you're sure you want to and you're not doing it because you think you should."

"I'll be there in a while."

He did come over, and Momma appeared worried. She was remembering how she fell for Daddy and the pain she'd suffered because of it.

Stan and I drove around for a while, and I started to cry. "What's wrong?" he said. "I thought you were over being mad at me."

"I'm not mad at you. I need you to tell me. Are you here because you care for me or not?"

Part III

Summer

Summer is the season that fosters maturity. Life progresses little by little as the days lazily unfold and progress. Time creeps stealthily by in the warm breezes, barely noticed until harvest wanders in.

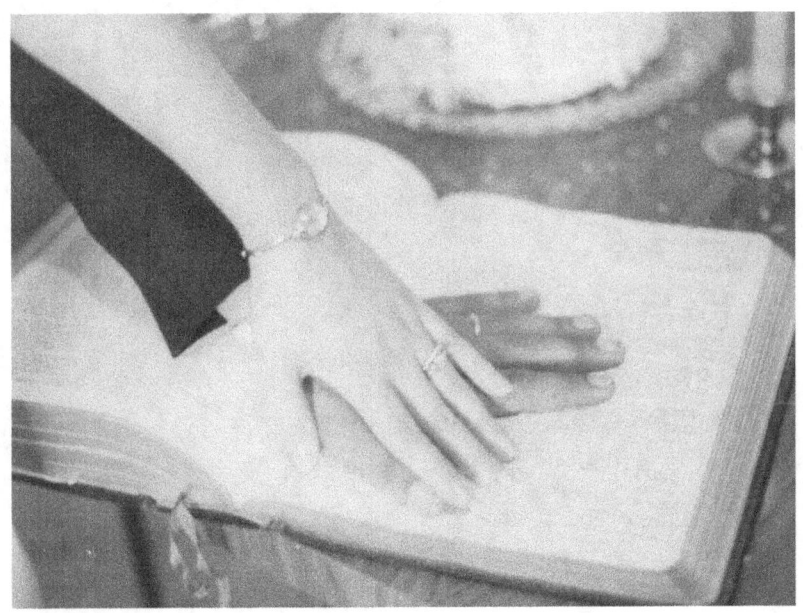

Chapter 12

"What do you think we should do?" Stan asked, panicking at the thought of becoming a daddy.

"I guess we need to get married," I said as terrified as he. "I mean, if that's what you want to do."

"Okay," Stan readily agreed, "we were going to get married anyway, so I guess we need to do it sooner than we thought. When do you want to do it?"

"Well, I suppose the sooner the better," I responded hopefully. "If we wait too long, people will gossip terribly. How about in two weeks? I need time to make my wedding dress and buy your wedding ring."

"Okay by me. The sooner we get this done the less nervous I'll be. I'll need to tell my mom. I'll be the first of her four boys to leave home. I'm not sure how happy she'll be."

A Few Days Later

"Stan, did you tell your mom yet? Was she upset?" I asked, anxious to know if his family would welcome me as a daughter-in-law.

"Well, she thought it was too soon and asked me if we were in trouble. I had to tell her the truth, and I told her we were planning to get married anyway. She asked me if I was sure the baby was mine. That's how moms are, I guess. I told her of course it's mine, and everything is just fine, but she's still worried."

"Oh." I hesitated. "She doesn't know me. I can understand her concern, but in time she will be okay with it, I hope."

Our wedding was small, only a few close friends and family members. The ceremony was held at Stan's parents' home. His uncle, a Baptist minister, performed the ceremony, and his cousin took the wedding pictures. Belinda was my matron of honor, and Jim was Stan's best man. Momma made the wedding cake, and Daddy gave me away. The entire wedding, including my self-made dress, Stan's wedding band, and the marriage license and paying the preacher, cost less than one hundred dollars. After the wedding we had less than three dollars and never gave it a second thought.

The next morning we woke up hungry. Then we thought about money. Across the street from the motel was a Krystal hamburger restaurant. Stan drove across the street and came back with two cups of coffee and one egg sandwich, which we shared. We were broke, except for pocket change.

"What will we do for dinner and supper?" Stan asked, worried about his stomach.

"Why don't we go home? We paid the rent for the mobile home and the cabinets are stocked with food. There's no need to go hungry when we have food at home." So we went home.

Our wedding was on Friday evening, and we went back to work on Monday. After work I prepared supper, and when we finished eating, Stan asked, "Did you buy any peanut butter?"

"Of course," I said. "It's in the cabinet above the sink."

"That little bitty jar—I ate that last night." Stan had an odd look as if there was something I should have known.

"You ate the whole jar?" I asked. Then I was the one with the odd look on my face. "Who eats that much peanut butter at one sitting? Momma always bought the small jar, and it lasted several weeks!"

"Your family must not like peanut butter," he laughed. "We always bought it in super-sized jars."

His love for peanut butter was the first amazing thing I learned about my new husband. The next time, I bought a huge jar of peanut butter, and every time we bought groceries, we bought more. None of it ever spoiled.

*****

"Belinda, may I come to your house and spend the day? I'm not feeling well. I think I might be in labor, but I'm not sure. How did you know when it was time to go? The doctor said since this was our first baby, there might be false labor."

"Of course you can come over here. Did you call Stan yet?"

"No, he's working, and I don't want to call him if it's not time."

"Come on over here, and I'll keep an eye on you, sis." Belinda was my only friend those days. My friends from high school had moved into the "I'm single and I'm free" lifestyle. It was not appealing to me. Stan and I were very happy, and now with our baby coming soon, it was hard to imagine a better lifestyle.

The pains kept coming, each one closer and harder. By midafternoon Belinda convinced me to call Stan. It was nearly time for his shift to end, so I called him and told him I was in labor. When he walked through the front door at Belinda's, he was so excited and nervous that he kept standing there, talking. "We should go," I said. "The pains are severe."

"I need a shower before we go. Do I have time?"

"I guess so. They say the first one takes longer, but don't be too long, okay?"

Stan went home to shower. He was gone for what seemed an eternity, and each pain was harder and more intense. Belinda and I were getting worried.

"Belinda, will you call him and see what's taking so long?" I groaned in agony, getting very upset because Stan wasn't back yet.

"He's on his way," Belinda said grinning.

"What's so funny?"

"Your sweet husband is so excited, he went to his mom and dad's to tell them the baby is coming and let the time get away. He'll be here in a minute." She laughed good-naturedly.

*****

"We're taking Mrs. Bristol downstairs to x-ray," the orderly said to Stan. "We need to see what's happening in there."

"What do you mean, what's happening?"

"We need to see if she is going to be able to deliver the baby."

"Mrs. Bristol, your baby is going to be a breech birth," Dr. Kingsley said, concern evident in his voice. "He's positioned with his bottom down where the head should be. He's too far into the birth canal for us to turn him or to do a caesarean."

"His head was down a few weeks ago," I said. "Then he did a complete rollover, but you told me he still had time to turn."

"We are not going to be able to give you the spinal you requested. Your baby needs you to be strong so you can help him be born. Can you do that, Maddie?"

"I'll try," the words shrieked out. The intensity of the spasm in my lower abdomen was in total control.

After thirteen hours of debilitating torture, Jasper was born, and the memory of the pain was washed away with tears of joy. When Stan called to tell Momma the news, she said, "Cal was a breech baby too. I sure hope he's not bottom side up for the rest of his life like his Grandpa."

At ages twenty and twenty-two, neither of us were experienced in rearing children, but we grabbed hold with both hands and held on tight. We had low-paying jobs. The better-paying ones went to people with higher education. Both of us had grown up making do with what we had, so we were satisfied with just making ends meet. It was enough.

Jasper stayed with my momma and daddy during the day while we worked. By age three he had bonded with both of them, tightly.

He thought his Papaw was super-duper, and I was thrilled Daddy was taking an interest in him. Jasper loved the farm, eating strawberries, feeding the cow, and riding with Papaw on the tractor. Everything seemed to be right, finally.

Stan had never seen the ocean, and we hadn't taken a vacation since we'd been married. We wanted to go to the beach, so Daddy said he could drive us and pay half the travel expense. We made our plans, and when the day came a few months later, the five of us set out for Panama City Beach, Florida. Stan, Jasper, and I were so excited we could hardly wait to get there.

Momma, Jasper, and I were riding in the backseat of Dad's car, while Stan and Dad were talking in the front. Partway into the drive she looked at me with sadness in her eyes and whispered. "Cal is leaving me again. As soon as we get back home, he's filing for divorce."

"*What?* Why? I didn't know anything was wrong. Have you been fighting? When did he tell you this?" I rambled on, hardly able to believe what she'd told me.

"He's been going to the Saturday night square dances with friends he used to work with in Oak Ridge. He knows I don't dance, so he never asked me to go. I got tired of staying home alone, so I got ready last Saturday night to go with him. He told me most emphatically I was not going, and he left without me. That's when I started to suspect he was being unfaithful."

"Oh, Momma, why didn't you tell me sooner? We don't need to go to the beach. You will be miserable." I spoke louder than I should, and she placed a finger across her lips. But I didn't want to be quiet. Cal never took responsibility for anything he did. I wanted him to know I knew, and I wanted him to know what I thought, but Momma said no, so I honored her wishes.

"He didn't tell me he wanted a divorce until right before we left to come to your house," she said. "You and Stan had been looking forward to this vacation for weeks, and I didn't want you to miss it. The only reason I'm telling you now is so you'll understand why we'll be staying in separate rooms at the hotel."

I was so angry I could have chewed nails. How could he do this to us, *again*?

Daddy put on his happy face and pretended all was well. Dad and I went shopping for souvenirs one afternoon and I hoped he would talk to me about it. Instead, he asked me to help him pick out a gift for "the office secretary." I said, "I never met her, so I don't know enough about her to pick out a gift for her." *Secretary, my foot!*

Traitor! Deceiver! Liar! Jerk! came to mind, with all the words I'd been taught never to say: *Dabby-Doo! Dabby-Doo! Dabby-Doo!* I wanted to go out on the beach, pick up the biggest pile of doggy doo I could find, and smear it across his two-timing face. But I didn't. I added it to my Pandora's Box full of repressed anger.

We left the beach a day early.

When we got back, Daddy packed his bags and left Momma. He never said a single word to Belinda or me, and he never said good-bye to Jasper or to Belinda's son, Mark.

Belinda was as angry as I was, and we did our best to spend more time with Momma so she wouldn't be alone.

Over the next few weeks Jasper still stayed with Momma during the day, but he couldn't understand why Papaw was gone. "Why did he leave us, Mamaw?" he asked her with big crocodile tears flowing from his eyes. Daddy had gone way too far this time. Hurting Momma, Belinda, and me was one thing; but hurting the grandchildren who thought he was the best ... now that was a whole different level of lowdown!

Daddy had obviously been planning on this long before he left. Before our beach vacation he found a buyer for the farm and started building a house in the same subdivision where Stan and I lived. He said he wasn't able to work the farm anymore and took a glass installation job in Oak Ridge. Two weeks after our vacation he came in with the divorce papers and told Momma she could keep the lot and the unfinished house. "Don't ask for alimony," he said. "I won't pay it. I've fulfilled my responsibility to you and the girls, now I'm going to go out and get everything I want."

When the bank statement came, Momma opened it as she always did. Right there in the envelope was a copy of a cancelled check, made payable to a jewelry store in North Carolina. It was dated on the same weekend he had packed up and left. The note in the memo section read "wedding rings." She couldn't believe what she was seeing. He had gone to North Carolina and married someone else before their divorce was even final!

Momma didn't have the money to finish building the house, so she traded it to the owner of our subdivision for a smaller lot and a used mobile home and moved in next door to us. We were happy she was close by us. At least she didn't have to be alone anymore.

Chapter 13

I remembered my earlier days in church and how important they had been to me. Those were the only days when peace and joy were the norm and not just passing shadows as in later years.

The old country church Momma, Belinda, and I attended before California was where we learned of God's plan of salvation, the heavenly eternity awaiting His children, and the fiery eternity awaiting those who rejected His precious gift. The old country preacher who proclaimed the gospel to us left a deep and influential imprint. I wanted that for our children.

Neither Stan nor I had been in church since we married. The years for training up Jasper under the godly influence of Christian ways were passing quickly. Belinda was raising her family in church and remained a constant reminder to me of how important it is to bring the children up right.

When Jasper was three, we started attending The Oaks Church where Stan's family had attended since he was a child. It was a small church full of love and devotion to Jesus, and everyone welcomed us. The Oaks Church is where I repented and renewed my commitment to God and where Stan accepted Jesus as his Savior. (I had accepted Him at age nine at Macedonia Baptist fourteen years earlier.)

Two years later our second child was born. Devon was bigger than I could deliver, so there were complications. The doctor told us to wait until the pains were three minutes apart before heading to the hospital. We waited, but the doctor still didn't show up at the hospital for his first progress check until several hours later. Meantime, the pains were coming fast and hard, but I wasn't progressing. The umbilical cord slipped off the baby's chin, choking him with every contraction. Doctors and nurses were gathered around the bed with instruments, forceps, and monitors, inserting scopes and wires into my body.

I was losing consciousness. Every time the room started to spin and go black, an ammonia stick under my nose brought me back. "Just a few more minutes, Maddie, I need you awake. Don't push until I tell you. You don't want to hurt the baby."

After minutes that seemed like hours, it was over. Devon and I both spent two days in the hospital so the doctors could watch him. His cord compression had choked him badly, but his color returned to normal, and he was fine.

Devon had digestive tract issues. Whether from the trauma during birth or some other reason, the outcome was stressful. Every time he ate, he vomited back half of it. He cried and cried every day for months after we brought him home.

One afternoon, when Devon had been crying off and on for eighteen hours and I was exhausted, we had a visitor. Near midafternoon a car pulled into our driveway and honked. I went to the door to see who was there, and what a surprise—though I can't say it was a pleasant one. Daddy's brother David had come by and brought Mossie to see her new great-grandson. They refused to get out of the car, so I walked out to see them.

I hadn't seen Mossie since Daddy sold the farm and left Momma. She had never been a typical grandmother to Belinda and me, neither when we were babies nor after Momma and Daddy remarried. Even when she lived in the same house with Daddy and Momma, and Jasper was spending his days with them, she never paid any attention to Jasper. I didn't understand why she was here now.

"I brought Mother by to see the baby," David said. "Can you bring him to the car? We don't plan to stay."

"I've just put him down for a nap. Why don't you come on in for a while? He doesn't usually sleep long until he's up and crying again."

"So you're not going to let me see the baby?" Mossie asked.

"It's not that I don't want you to see him, Mossie. He's sick and been awake for over eighteen hours. If I bring him out, it will wake him, and he needs to rest." I was as polite as I could manage while biting my tongue.

"Well, I was going to give him this dollar for his piggy bank, but I guess you don't want that either?" She turned her nose up and let go a heavy breath, like a bull about to charge.

"I'm sorry, Mossie. Of course I'll put the dollar in his piggy bank, and I'll help you out of the car and into the house, if you will just come in for a while."

"No, we'll go." She beamed at David and said, "I'm ready to go." David looked at me apologetically, put the car in reverse, and they left.

When you've spent your first ten years in a warm, loving environment, with God as the authority figure, and the second ten years under the oppressive hand of an earthly father, it's hard to discern what you are. Are you a child of God who should lean on His everlasting promises? Or are you just an object of circumstance to be tolerated by the powers that be? I was soon to know the answer.

Nine months after Devon was born, I became pregnant again. The moment I found out, I cried. Jasper's birth was breech, Devon's came with complications, and I was just not strong enough to go through another traumatic experience so soon. Stan encouraged me and loved me through the shock, but still it was more than I could cope with physically or emotionally without help. So I called on my heavenly Father.

> Dear Father,
>
> Our children are wonderful blessings from You, and I love them so much. I thank You, Lord, for the two we have and for the one growing in my womb. My body is weak from stress and so tired from caring for both of them. I don't believe I can

do this again. Please, Father, if it's Your will, please make this one small enough so there aren't any complications and turned head down, so it's not breech. I love You, Father. Whatever is Your will, I trust You will do what is needed.

Amen

Eight and a half months later, on an early Saturday morning, the labor pains started. Momma came to our house to sit with the boys, and we took our time driving to the hospital. The first two deliveries took nearly twelve hours each, so we saw no reason to rush. Less than an hour after we left home we were checked into the hospital and were in the maternity ward, getting ready for a long and agonizing day.

The nurse came in and asked if I wanted something for pain. "Sure," I said, "I've been through this twice before, and it will likely be a while." She went to get the shot of pain reliever, and before she came back, my water broke. She gave me the shot and checked to see how much farther we had to go before dilation was complete.

"Sweetie, you're crowning! We are taking you to delivery!" Two or three hard pushes later, Helena was born. Stan thought the doctor was mistaken.

"We just got here," Stan said, "and we always have boys!"

The doctor laughed and said, "Not this time, Mr. Bristol. You are the daddy of a five pound and seven ounce beauty."

Tears rolled across my cheeks from joy, relief, and praise to my heavenly father when the nurse said, "If she had been one ounce lighter we would have called her a preemie and kept her a few days for observation." Then I knew: God had heard and answered my prayer. I am a child of God, and I can lean on His everlasting promises. We went home from the hospital the next morning.

Although we attended church regularly and were involved in church works, something was still empty inside me. God's Word was chock-full of promises and assurances to His children who sought after Him wholeheartedly; but I didn't see that in our lives. There had to be something we were missing, something more than attending church and trying to do what God said was the right things: honesty, truth, patience, kindness, and walking in the straight path He laid out for us in the Bible. I was hungry for more.

Matthew 7:7, in the King James Version (KJV), says, "Ask, and it shall be given you; seek, and ye shall find; knock, and it shall be opened unto you."

That promise started me on a spiritual journey and a strong and wonderful personal relationship with God Himself.

> Dear Father,
> You promised many things to Your children, and I want to believe every one of them; but I just don't see them. I need to know that I know that I know You are who the Bible says You are. I'm so tired of wanting to believe it but yet not seeing it in action. My heart believes, but my head is struggling. If Your Word is true, then I want to embrace it fully and experience all that You are. Otherwise, I am laying it aside.
>
> Amen

The *amen* was barely out of my mouth when the Holy Spirit touched me as I'd never experienced it. A warm, intense *swoosh* started at my toes and swept throughout my entire body, nearly taking away my breath. Tears cascaded over my cheeks, and joy filled me to overflowing. The entire experience lasted only seconds, but when I came to myself, I was standing tiptoe in front of the refrigerator with arms stretched toward heaven and shouts of praise rolling from within my soul.

From then on, I never doubted His power. I set out on a spiritual quest and experienced the wonderment of God's love.

Hours and hours I spent digging into the Word of God, searching out promises and the conditions of receiving them. Seminars, sermons, books, tapes, and videos of God's people teaching and explaining, brought me full circle back to the foundational principles Jesus taught to his disciples.

> Love the Lord with all your being; love your neighbor as much as you love yourself. Trust in the Lord, and He will guide you.

Chapter 14

We had neither seen nor heard from Daddy since he had left three years earlier. None of us knew where he lived or even had a phone number to call. Out of the blue, he pulled into my driveway at Christmastime with his financially secure wife. (Her former husband had retired from the nuclear plants in Oak Ridge and left her with a cushy retirement plan when he died.)

I didn't know whether to open the door or run and hide. Bitterness, resentment, anger, and hatred smothered me until I could hardly breathe. I should have refused to let him in without an apology, but he came bearing gifts for our newborn baby girl. I could hardly refuse him a visit with his granddaughter. As difficult as it was, I couldn't bring myself to inflict on him the same pain of rejection he brought to us. So I invited them to come in for a visit. He gave me a stuffed puppy dog for Helena but brought nothing for Jasper or Devon. Devon was twenty months old, so I gave the dog to him. He and the dog became inseparable. Jasper didn't care about getting a gift from a stranger.

No words could describe the awkwardness of that introduction. Henrietta, his wife, didn't know what type of man she'd married. She was a good-hearted woman who would never hurt anyone voluntarily. Daddy led her to believe he and Mom had been divorced for years. I couldn't dislike her, but neither could I welcome her as a family member. Daddy conducted himself as if everything was good between us. For Henrietta's sake, I let her believe it.

They stayed only a few minutes, just long enough to stir up my troubled heart. I will never understand how he'd lived his entire life under false pretenses, and now he was expecting me to do the same. One more trinket was added to my vault of suppressed emotions. A volcano was rumbling.

The next time I heard from him was more than a year later when I received a Christmas card from Bellflower, California. Desperate for answers and closure, I wrote him a letter and begged him to tell me why. He never responded.

*****

Momma was never one to go to the doctor. If she was sick she toughed it out with home remedies and over-the-counter drugs. The only time she went to a doctor was when Belinda was born and then only on the day of the birth. Once when we were in California, she and I were hit by a car while crossing the street in a pedestrian crosswalk. A driver who was not paying attention ran through the stop and bumped both of us to the ground. My injury was minor, but Momma had several deep bruises and suffered much pain from it. She went to the emergency room to be checked for broken bones, but she hadn't been to a doctor since. Doctors made her nervous, so she didn't go unless it was life or death.

This time it was just that. She found a lump under her left arm, and we insisted she go let a doctor check it. She had cancer in her lymph nodes and both her breasts. It had advanced beyond the point of surgery.

"How bad is it, Doctor?" Belinda and I asked, dreading to hear the diagnosis.

"I won't lie to you," he said. "With no treatment, she has maybe two or three months; with treatment, maybe two years. Is she covered by insurance?"

"No," we both responded. "She doesn't even have income except for what we pay her for child care."

"Her options are limited," he said. "I won't charge her for today, but before I can treat her, she will need a means of payment. There are agencies that help indigent patients, but they only pay for minimum treatments. I'll get you the information for applying. Whenever you get her payment secured, call me and we will set up an appointment for her first chemotherapy session."

As is anyone whenever they get bad news, we were devastated, angry, and not willing to accept the verdict. It couldn't be so far advanced; she'd only found the lump a few weeks ago. Stan, eleven-year-old Jasper, six-year-old Devon, five-year-old Helena, and I knelt side by side on our living room floor and prayed. This time there was no peaceful relief.

During the last two months of Momma's illness, my employer gave me a leave of absence from my job. Belinda came by our house every day, and together we cared for Momma. By then, Daddy was back in Tennessee trying to make a spot for himself in our lives. He came by one day to see Momma. I led him into the bedroom where she was resting and left him alone with her.

He sat in the room with her for a while and then came out quietly. "I've always loved your mother," he said. That was just not true. Love is not self-serving.

"Why did you leave him in here with me?" Momma asked, almost angrily, after he was gone.

"I thought he might have something he needed to say to you, Momma. I didn't mean to offend you."

"He didn't say anything."

Two weeks later Momma was gone. She was fifty-eight.

I tried to go back to work afterward and did work for a few weeks. When the shock began to subside, the reality of the last two months came crashing down around me. I had read how stress was a major factor in many types of cancer, and I blamed Daddy for Momma's death. Her entire life had been a huge ball of stress brought on by his actions. He left her without food, money, or means of support; he disrespected her, he verbally abused her, and then he left her again. I couldn't forgive him.

An entire year passed before life eased back into a new routine. It was a year of questioning, reflection, healing, and growing closer to God.

Collection of Thoughts and Memories

Today felt like 1960, a touch of fall was in the air.
I was a child out playing in the backyard without care.
I could see my mother standing on the back porch with a broom.
Her wispy hair was falling 'round her face. She hummed a tune.
So happy in my childhood I can remember still,
The sweet taste of corn and butter; I could never eat my fill.
A huge cane-bottomed rocker so big I could not reach
The plank floored porch beneath it as I sat upon its seat.
I can hear the rooster crowing and frogs croaking in the pond.
An old white dog named Snowball lies sleeping in the sun.
The taste of ripe persimmons so bittersweet, yet good;
Drawing water from the cistern and chopping kindling wood.
A playhouse in the woods with imaginary walls,
A grapevine used for swinging and a stuffed sock for a ball.
All these things so very vivid in my mind today because
It felt like 1960 and the air so smelled like fall.
So many thoughts and memories at rest within my soul,
Lying silently awaiting their glories to unfold.
When next I chance to wander through the meadows of my mind
As the smells and touch of autumn take me back again, in time.

Chapter 15

When I was a child, people asked me what I wanted to be when I grew up. I always said, "I want to work in an office."

"You want to be a secretary?" someone asked.

"No! I don't want any man telling me what to do. I want to work with numbers"—not knowing what the accounting profession was called.

After high school graduation I went straight to work as a receptionist for my cousins in their glass installation business. I wanted to go to Knoxville Business College, but our small-town high school didn't help seniors with financial aid for college. I had no money, and Daddy said, "A college education would be wasted on a girl. She'll just end up raising babies anyway."

Our friend Charles from church suggested I apply for a job at the state university. I told him I had tried once before, but the university jobs were nearly always filled before they even made it to the jobs board at Union County job services. Current employees of the state always got first dibs on open positions, and many were filled even before the required posting period expired.

"You go to the personnel office at the university and fill in a basic application," Charles said. "Call me when it's done. I know people there who owe me favors. If you go, I will give them your name. I can't control the outcome, but if you have the necessary skills, I can help you get an interview."

I went, and I got a job as an accounts payable clerk. There were two managers in the office: one in accounting and one in purchasing. The accounting manager with whom I interviewed was a woman of class and somewhat intimidating to a country girl wearing used clothing. Unaware of the "what not to wear for a job interview" code, I wore my best dress, but it was not navy and cream. She hired me anyway.

A few weeks later the accounting manager moved into another position, and I ended up working for the purchasing manager. Later, after we had worked together for several years, she told me she was glad the accounting manager hired me; but if the final decision had been hers on the day I interviewed, she would not have hired me, because my outfit was not proper for a job interview. God always goes ahead of His children, preparing the way before them. The Science Business Office at the state university was where God wanted me to be.

*****

I asked God to teach me to love the unlovely and to help me understand why Daddy made such painful choices. If I could understand, maybe I could find a way to love him.

In my mind I was ready to move full speed ahead spreading the news of God's love. I wasn't ready, and God knew it. My heart was still full of bitterness, resentment, and unresolved anger for my daddy, and God couldn't use me in that condition.

Early one morning, before I headed out the door for work, sorrow overpowered me. Deep, deep pangs of anguish rumbled in my soul like the roar of a volcano nearing eruption. The mass of pain, anger, bitterness, and hatred was going to explode from inside the vault I thought I'd buried so deep it could never find the light of day.

On the way to work, my mind went soaring back through the years, reliving, remembering, and begging for relief. As my car approached the road leading to Daddy's place, I turned into it. He was married to a local woman now, who owned the neighborhood market. Henrietta had discarded him when her children threatened to kill him. They refused to give him any part of their daddy's estate and were ready to kill him to keep him from getting it. Henrietta put him out of the house and refused to let him come back.

I had no idea what to say to him, but I needed to see him. I pulled into the store parking lot, and Daddy stepped out like he had been waiting for me. God was directing this meeting; otherwise Daddy would not have been outside so early in the morning. The store was not yet open.

He opened the passenger door of the car and sat down, looked at me, and waited. Words started to flow from me, words I'd never planned on saying.

"Daddy, I need you to forgive me," I blubbered through the tears.

"Why do you need my forgiveness? You haven't done anything to me."

"I hated you for over thirty years, and I need you to forgive me for it. Why did you do those things, Daddy?"

Broken and leaning into the relief of confession, Daddy sobbed mournfully and said, "Just selfishness, I guess. Can you ever forgive me?"

It was what I needed. He'd finally acknowledged it. Now I had closure.

"Yes, Daddy, I believe I can now. I'll try." Hugging each other, this time with love, we cried together. The festering corruption from harboring years of bitterness, resentment, anger, and hate so deeply embedded in my heart poured out and then dwindled before finally settling into remission. Forgiveness set both of us free.

Chapter 16

My job at the state university afforded us many benefits which otherwise would have been beyond our means. College tuition was free, up to two classes per year. Certifications were available to those who met the qualifications for taking the exams. A certification achieved came with a raise. Four years into my short-lived employment at the university, a yen to work with the public kept calling me to get a better education. My job gave great benefits but not much opportunity to work directly with people. I mostly did paperwork from a tiny office in the basement of the Peavey Science Building, where the only thing visible from the window was students' feet passing by on their way to class.

The wonderful lady who supervised our office encouraged those working under her to take advantage of the educational opportunities available as part of our benefits package. Until then, the lack of self-confidence and lack of funding had held me back from pursuing higher education. Thanks to her encouragement and the university benefits, both those barriers were gone.

A few college classes, job certification, and a good raise inspired bigger hopes. A few tax preparation classes and a part-time seasonal job with a major tax preparation chain opened a door. The world said that door would never be opened to me because I hadn't earned a college degree, but God is the one who opens and shuts doors for those who follow Him.

As far back as my memory reached, public bookkeeping was only a dream until God made it a reality. A retiring elderly gentleman offered me an opportunity to buy out his home-based bookkeeping service. We had no money other than a small cash value in a life insurance policy. No bank was willing to lend us money to buy a business with neither of us having any experience in business management. Stan and I didn't see it happening and pushed the thought away without looking into it further. It continued to nag at me.

A few weeks later, the gentlemen called me up and asked me if I was interested. The year was flying by, and he needed an answer. "I'll give you until Friday to tell me your decision," he said. "Then I'll need to withdraw the offer until after tax season. I sold the tax division of my business to another buyer and promised to work for them until the April fifteenth filing deadline. If you don't want the bookkeeping service, I need to make other arrangements."

Stan and I talked it over again. "You want this, don't you?" he said.

"It's something I've always wanted, but there are so many things to consider," I pointed out. "My job at the university has good benefits, especially the health insurance. The pay is better than any job I've ever had. Maybe we could come up with the small price he's asking for the business by cashing in the life insurance policy and borrowing money on our credit cards. If it doesn't work out, I will have given up my job, and we would have no way to pay it back. Plus, the income represented by the financial statements is less than what I am making now. There's no guarantee 100 percent of the clients will stay on when I take over the business."

Unable to make a decision and afraid of passing up a once-in-a-lifetime opportunity, we prayed for guidance. When Friday came, I still had no peace with moving forward or staying. While returning books to the university library, I felt prayer seeping from my soul. As I walked, I prayed, "Father, I need Your help. Please show me what to do. Whether You want me to stay where I am or move on, Your will is what I'm asking."

As I passed through the glass doors of the library and started down the steps, a glorious vision enveloped me. The world faded into hazy dreamlike fog, and a dark gulf lay in front of me. Across the gulf a hand was extended toward me. I heard a crisp, concise voice speak to my spirit. "It's okay. Come on over."

As quickly as it came, it was gone. The entire event lasted no more than the time it took for one step. My body was shaking, my legs trembling, and my head in a spin. Tears flooded my eyes, blurring my vision. I descended the steps, cautiously clutching the hand rails, and walked across the street to a bench beside a water fountain. Unable to hold myself steady, I sat there, trying to gain control; and trying not to attract the attention of passersby. I don't know how long I sat there, but I knew eventually someone would come looking for me if I didn't get back to the office soon.

The answer was there. As soon as I got back to my office, I headed straight to my supervisor and told her my plans. She congratulated me and encouraged me onward. On the way home that evening, I told Stan about the spiritual experience at the library. We accepted the vision as confirmation of God's plan for us, embraced it fully, and never looked back.

Whenever God makes plans for your advancement in His holy kingdom, testing and trying precedes the promotion. Just as Jesus was led into the wilderness to be tempted by Satan, so must we be as well. Jesus was well aware He was the Son of God, and He was strong in that truth. That was the strength Satan tried to destroy. The same is true for God's children. The areas where we believe ourselves to be strongest can ultimately be our weakest points.

Once the business became ours, it was time to get busy. I jumped into action full throttle, inspired and motivated by the opportunity before me. Shyness and low self-confidence always plagued me at the beginning of any new job, but this time was different. Never had I experienced such ease of transition. God gave me new confidence and boldness. I felt professional.

Satan didn't wait too long to stick his nose into God's business. Stan and I had been a solid team for nearly twenty-five years, and nothing in the world could have convinced me I could be tempted to stray. Still, temptation came.

If anyone had ever told me I could be tempted by covetousness and lust, I would have laughed them to shame. "You don't know me very well if you think that could ever happen to me." I would have boasted. Satan knew me much better than I knew myself. The business was ours for less than a month when Satan came knocking. A subtle nudge, a gentle whisper, a tiny hint of a pleasant aroma; those are the things he presents to us in packages so innocently wrapped, the lure is completely concealed. He catches innocent prey off guard in an unsuspecting moment and leads them away from safety with poisoned bait masquerading as wholesome fruit.

Temptation stopped in daily, and each day the lure was more appealing. Beyond the temptation stood an open door, an escape route. To get to the escape route, I had to turn my back on temptation. I refused to turn.

For two years my heart was torn between what was good and right and what Satan said was good and right. Satan teased the flame the way a gentle breeze teases a candle, stirring the fire but never allowing it to be extinguished. We played games, Satan and I, until I was so weak I was ready to give him the win. At my weakest moment, when Satan was ready to claim the glory, Jesus stepped into the midst.

"Don't bother people with those tracts," the little girl's mother said to her in the market.

"But Mommy," the little girl pleaded as she passed the tract to me with a great big smile, "the Sunday school teacher said we need to pass them out."

"It's okay," I said to the mother. "I'm happy to take one."

As I walked away from the girl and her mommy, I stared at the tract in my hand. In big, bold, letters, screaming for my attention was a message sent just to me: "Someday, you will have to face God."

My heart caved, but my spirit rejoiced. Jesus stood as a beacon shining through the door of escape, pulling me toward it with warming intensity. I turned my back on temptation, and the victory was won.

To quote my brother-in-law, "You mustn't ask for it unless you really want it." God answers the prayers that bring us into alignment with His perfect will. I had asked to understand why. He let me experience a touch of what Daddy struggled with throughout his entire life, all because he refused to take the escape route.

I confessed my temptations to Stan and begged his forgiveness. Even though he did not know my thoughts, and people might say telling him made it worse, God said differently. Some might argue that lust is not sin until it's conceived. Jesus said looking upon others to lust after them is adultery of the heart. My heart belonged to Stan—it always had and always will—but harboring secrets and living under the weight of lies and deception nearly destroyed my soul once. I couldn't let it happen again. God does not allow prosperity when sin is unconfessed and unforgiven. I had to tell Stan even if it meant he never trusted me again.

Time heals all wounds, or so it's said. Although wounds are healed by time, scars can be ever visible as a constant reminder. A betrayal of the heart does not heal overnight, and trust is slow to return; but when God heals wounds, scars gently fade away.

Part IV

Autumn

The time of year when crops are harvested, cupboards and barns are full, and nature's colors are arrayed in an astonishing exhibition. A time for reflection: a time to share the bounty: and a time to prepare for the winter ahead.

Chapter 17

Climbing and climbing, out of breath, I must stop here for a while; then I'll go higher. I've climbed to the sixteenth floor. There are several more floors to go before I've seen everything. The first fifteen were filled with priceless antiques and treasures. This one has only one good piece. The space is small and dirty, with cobwebs hanging everywhere. Aaah, a balcony with rocking chairs: A place to rest.

What a peaceful, serene, tropical paradise, out beyond the balcony. The river flows from somewhere up above, gently rocking the boats as they glide downstream.

From behind me, a voice—familiar, yet not—invites, "Sit; rest awhile. We'll talk."

"Now, there is the place where I want to go," I say out loud to the figure rocking back and forth on the chair in the shadows.

"You shall, but not today. Go back inside and look around the room. You will not climb higher. The doors to the upper rooms are locked. You will stay here and work. Everything here is yours."

Back inside, I try the door to the upward staircase. It is locked. I should head back down now; but no, I'm compelled to stay. I look around the room and see a soiled but lovely antique rocking chair. Even in its sullied condition its value is unmistakable. I can restore it, and then I can take my ease until time to go.

No, not yet. There will be time for that later. The old white medicine cabinet on the wall next to the stairwell draws my attention. The doors are sagging; the hinges are broken. It needs to be repaired; but I can't fix it. I don't have the skills.

Gently, painstakingly, I remove the cabinet from the wall and carry it into the room to my right. There are many windows, and the lighting is very good. It's a workshop. I'll leave the cabinet here.

Beep, beep, beep, beep—louder and louder, the alarm on the night table blares, shattering the dream into oblivion.

Wide awake now, I scurry around the room, getting ready for another day. Every day I've grown more tired and less motivated. The workload from the business has grown beyond my ability to handle it alone. Several employees have come and stayed a few years before moving on to higher-paying jobs where they could advance beyond clerical positions.

A few years back we moved my office from the rented office space in town to our converted carport. I have been working from home, so finding help is difficult. Employment agencies have refused to work with me because of the risks involved with sending someone to a personal residence.

*****

I was tired, and there appeared to be no relief coming soon. Even if I could find the help I needed, getting them trained and ready for the busy tax filing season ahead would be next to impossible if it didn't happen by November. October was speeding by, and it looked as if I would be disappointing many people this year. I would have to cut back and work only for the few clients who came to me every month for bookkeeping services. It was not what I wanted, but it was okay if it had to be. What I wanted most was the opportunity to pass along to someone else the grace God had given me: to help someone else realize a dream through reliance on God's promises.

I'd been praying often, asking God to send me help or to tell me if it was time to pull back and go at a slower pace. Belinda needed a job, so she came to work for me, helping with household chores and cooking, which tremendously lightened my overall workload, but there was not even a hint of wisdom to help me decide what to do with the business.

There was the situation at the church. Membership was down to just a few elderly members who had been attending church there for many, many years. "There's no giving up," the patient few contended. "This church has been through tough times in the past. God will intervene if we just wait."

The calling in my heart to teach was strong—to share the things God had done for me throughout my fifty-plus years. Stan was a deacon, and I played piano for the congregational singing. We had ties, duties, and commitments to fulfill but little opportunity to teach and share outside our small circle. I wanted to move forward and maybe even move on to another church where there were young people. I needed to be teaching: but there was not an inkling of change anywhere in sight.

The dream kept tugging at my mind, bothering me the way a child refuses to go unnoticed. It just kept pulling on the skirt of my consciousness until I paid attention. What could it mean? Was it significant, or was it just my subconscious telling me I needed to rest?

Finally my mind was made up. "I'm not looking any further for bookkeeping and income tax help," I said, both to myself and to God. "If You want me to continue on in the direction I've been going, I trust You to send me the help I need. Unless You specifically direct me otherwise, I'm going to find a church where I can get busy teaching others of Your love."

One day, from out of the blue our daughter, Helena, called me and told me she had a friend who needed a job. "She's so much like you, Mom. You two will get along well together, I'm sure."

"I do need help," I said. "But I need someone who can grab hold of the ball and keep it bouncing without needing a lot of instruction. There's hardly enough time before the busy months to train someone from scratch."

"Jill has worked as a bank teller and as an office manager for a company that went out of business," Helena said. "She won't need very much training."

"Well, if she's interested, tell her to come by my office one day. It surely won't hurt to check her out, but I'm not too hopeful at this late date."

A Few Days Later

"Hello, are you Mrs. Bristol? I'm Jill." She was a picture of professionalism, and her countenance displayed confidence.

"Come on in, and please, you can call me Maddie. I'm happy to meet you. Helena says you're looking for a job, and I'm looking for help. Maybe we can help each other."

I reviewed her résumé and said, "I won't waste too much of your time though. I'll tell you what I'm looking for, and if you're still interested, we can talk business.

"The position requires someone who is dedicated enough to work long hours from January first through April fifteenth every year. The rest of the year the work load is heavy for two weeks out of every month. During the slow days we take time off to make up for the longer hours during tax filing time. I need someone who can take on half of the bookkeeping right away and the other half later and is willing to learn to be an income tax preparer.

"I'm over fifty years old. Not far up the road I hope to pass this business on to someone who can keep it going. In short, I'm looking for a professionally minded, career-oriented person who wants to be independently employed."

Jill's eyes widened as she swallowed hard, trying not to appear overwhelmed. "I've handled a busy office with several employees where I was the full-charge bookkeeper. I've never been independently employed, and I'm not sure if I want to be. I never gave it any thought. I want to learn income tax preparation, and I do love a good challenge. You're not retiring soon, are you?"

"No," I said, realizing I'd shaken her confidence. "I didn't mean to suggest you would be on your own right away. The past few years have been frustrating for me. Every time I'm sure I've found someone who is dependable and trustworthy, they prove otherwise. I just wanted to be straight with you up front. If you're only interested in a job and not a career, there's no need for either of us to waste our time."

"I understand," Jill replied.

We talked job details, qualifications, experience, salary, and other routine interview essentials. After we'd covered every question and answer from both perspectives, I said, "If you want the job and accept the requirements, it's yours. When can you start?"

"I tell you what," she said confidently. "Why don't I come on board for now? Let me get used to the possibility of independent employment for the future. I'll need to pray. If that will work for you, I can start at the beginning of next week." Jill was a woman after my own heart, a prayer warrior.

By the time April 15 rolled around there was no doubt in either of our minds that God had brought us together. We worked together as if we had been at it for twenty years. There was none of the usual adjustments for personal comforts. We blended and complemented one another like chocolate and peanut butter. Jill jumped into the job, self-motivated, self-disciplined, and determined. Her work ethic surpassed any I expected. It didn't take me long to realize she was dependable, trustworthy, and extremely intelligent. The clients loved her and soon began calling in and asking for her. I couldn't have been more satisfied, and she enjoyed the work. Again God was fulfilling another of His wonderful promises, found in Proverbs 3:6 (KJV): "In all thy ways acknowledge him, and he shall direct thy paths."

Chapter 18

The dream still lurked in the back of my mind, hovering, waiting for acknowledgement. The harmonious merger with Jill confirmed it. My work with the business was not finished yet. So there must be another reason for the dream; otherwise, why was it still haunting me?

The Oaks Church was still meandering along with the few devoted members. The pastor was weary and done-in. Stan and I were ready to throw in the towel and move, but we could never bring ourselves to do it. We felt as if we were running away, cutting out when the battle became demanding. So we stayed. I needed, as usual, to know why. While I was praying and begging God to help us through this barren time, He gave me an understanding of the purpose of The Oaks Church through this:

Ivy and Oaks

A refuge, a sanctuary, an oasis.
Weary travelers pass through on their way to destiny.
They dwell for a while and then move on
Refreshed, restored.
Many have matured, grown strong like oaks,
Then departed, dropping acorns along the way.
Acorns embedded beneath the trailing ivy
Sprout forth from among the vines
Reaching for the sun. Another oak is born.
An oasis in the midst of a dry and desolate land;
Life is sustained, refreshed, renewed.
Where the wanderer returns home,
Remembering, recovering, resuscitating.
Be not weary when passing through desolation.
For the time will be when the wanderer will again pass by.

Chapter 19

I can't leave you without a reminder. God's conditional promises shall forever be available to His daughters and sons for as long as grace remains if we meet the humble conditions for receiving them.

The Holy Bible is full of promises, wisdom, understanding, blessings, and the only truly good things on this side of the mountain. I will guide you to a few of them, but I'm not going to tell you where to find them all. I want you to experience knowing God as Daddy, so I'll let you search for Him in His Word. All of it is conditional. We must seek Him, we must believe Jesus is the Christ, and we must meet His humble conditions for receiving.

Six Great and Precious Promises

Condition:	In all thy ways acknowledge him.
Promise:	And he shall direct thy paths (Proverbs 3:5–6).
Condition:	Honor thy father and thy mother.
Promise:	That thy days may be long upon the land which the Lord thy God giveth thee (Exodus 20:12).
Condition:	Give.
Promise:	And it shall be given unto you; good measure, pressed down, and shaken together, and running over shall men give into your bosom (Luke 6:38).
Condition:	Ask.
Promise:	And it shall be given you (Luke 11 9).
Condition:	Seek.
Promise:	And ye shall find (Luke: 11:9).
Condition:	Knock.
Promise:	And it shall be opened unto you (Luke 11:9).

Part V

Winter

Winter is the time when everything passes from life unto death for a short span. Hope sleeps silent and still, waiting for spring to warm the air and bring to fruition the assurance of eternal life.

Chapter 20

There's a chill in the air now. Autumn is almost past. I'm standing on the back porch looking across the way to the barren trees covering the ridges and foothills. The autumn sun casts a shadow on the valley below, reminding me winter is around the bend. Snow will soon cover the mountaintop, and the north wind will shortly usher in the cold. In the meantime, maybe I'll take a second look at restoring that old antique rocking chair; or perhaps I'll find a few broken white cabinets to carry into the light. We will continue on until life goes to sleep for a time, to wait for the newness of spring which will quicken the silent souls and restore all things anew.

Surely winter will not prolong her stay.

Epilogue

After Daddy and I had our confessional, our relationship was easier. We never did develop a daddy–daughter relationship; it was way too late for that, but we were friends. Our conversations were easy and open. Holidays and special occasions were no longer strained. He suffered through two open heart surgeries and eventually died from chronic heart disease. A passerby found him in his car by the side of the road where he had pulled over and stopped. He died alone. I was able to let him go, knowing that even though his physical heart was damaged, his spiritual heart was healed.

Granny Nettie passed away at age eighty-six. Before she died, she had a leg amputated as a consequence of diabetes.

Mossie lived to be in her nineties. She never became a part of our children's lives.

Uncle Ronnie passed away from a heart attack. He died on my birthday while digging sprouts from a flowering bush he wanted to share with Momma.

Aunt Minnie lived into her nineties and left a legacy of faith to everyone who met her. Her house is still standing, full of her things, just the way she left them. If any one of her family and friends wants to go back and remember the days we spent there while growing up, at family reunions, and while dining on those delicious dinners she prepared for every holiday, we can. She loved to cook, and she prepared for each of her children and grandchildren their favorite dish at every celebration. Her table was a feast of love.

Jill purchased our bookkeeping and income tax service business in October 2013—just as God had it planned. She is growing in leaps and bounds and giving God the glory for her success. Her continued success is a wonderful blessing to me.

Jim passed away in his sleep at age sixty-five after spending the evening with his and Belinda's children and grandchildren.

Belinda is still my best friend, and she still inspires me to walk with God daily. She sings gospel music with her new husband, Evan, and they spend their time helping others. Belinda has three children and five grandchildren.

Stan is still my precious, godly, and loving husband. We have walked through this life together, in good health and prosperity. It is our hope God will keep us the same way through far reaching days to come. We have three wonderful children and three treasured grandchildren. The grandchildren call him Pap. I'm Granny.

The Oaks Church is still standing and is now going strong. Several years ago when I prayed for God to help me be sure He truly called me to teach, I kept asking when. Our church attendance was down to a few faithful members who had been on the road with Christ for more years than I. He answered me in spirit with "When the remnant is gone, and the tenth returns." Today, most of the founding members are gone on to be with our Lord, and a few of their offspring returned to The Oaks Church. A true man of God now pastors our church, and a group of young Christians attend regularly. I am so glad I waited on God; for the youth class I am now teaching is a far greater blessing to me than I could ever be to them.

What more can I say? I am blessed, spoiled, and treated like royalty by my family and most especially by God Himself. He truly has been my Daddy, and I'm looking forward to the day when I can see Him face to face.